"I have a plan," Erin said

Brady folded his arms trying to remain in control of the situation. Only, just looking at Erin kept him aroused. "A plan?"

"I was thinking that neither of us really has time for a relationship. But that doesn't mean we don't have...needs." She reached up and toyed with his collar. "I thought we both could use a release valve. One with no strings, no demands. Just a safe outlet."

Brady knew there was nothing safe about Erin Mahoney. Not intellectually and sure as hell not sexually. And yet even as he stood there trying to convince himself he should turn her down, he knew he wouldn't.

So he didn't. Reaching for her, he crushed her lips with his. His hands slid over her curves, his fingers brushing the sides of her breasts as she moaned softly. He settled his hands on her hips, lifting her up. "Wrap your legs around me," he said in a husky voice as he carried her toward the bedroom. "Because I've got some plans of my own...."

Dear Reader,

I've always been a sucker for a cop story. The suspense, the drama, the fight for justice. Probably because I'm the daughter of a cop and have been a witness to that life for most of my own. Of course, as I got older, I wanted romance to go along with the suspense and drama. The rugged, hard-nosed detective who gets his man…and then gets his woman! In my case, I got what I wanted, both in the books I read and wrote, and in real life. In fact, it was while researching a story that I met my husband. He's not a hard-nosed detective, but I was just as captivated by him as a SWAT team commander.

I hope you're a sucker for a good cop story, too. I think you'll enjoy watching Erin Mahoney shake up hard-nosed homicide detective Brady O'Keefe. And I know you'll enjoy seeing just how Brady gets his woman.

Happy reading!

Donna Kauffman

P.S. I love to hear from readers.
Check out my Web site at www.donnakauffman.com.

Books by Donna Kauffman

HARLEQUIN TEMPTATION
828—WALK ON THE WILD SIDE

HEAT OF THE NIGHT
Donna Kauffman

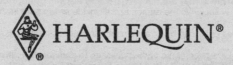

HARLEQUIN®

TORONTO • NEW YORK • LONDON
AMSTERDAM • PARIS • SYDNEY • HAMBURG
STOCKHOLM • ATHENS • TOKYO • MILAN • MADRID
PRAGUE • WARSAW • BUDAPEST • AUCKLAND

This book is dedicated to my Lawman.

ISBN 0-373-25946-8

HEAT OF THE NIGHT

Copyright © 2001 by Donna Jean.

This edition published by arrangement with Harlequin Books S.A.

® and TM are trademarks of the publisher. Trademarks indicated with ® are registered in the United States Patent and Trademark Office, the Canadian Trade Marks Office and in other countries.

Visit us at www.eHarlequin.com

Printed in U.S.A.

1

"THE HANDCUFFS and leather mask could be explained in any number of ways." Bill Henley swiveled his chair around and gazed out his office window. Fog still hugged the streets of Philadelphia, but Mayor Henley probably wasn't thinking about traffic jams or whether the mist would burn off before his nine o'clock tee off time.

Homicide detective Brady O'Keefe waited impatiently for Henley to come to terms with reality. The mayor was right about the handcuffs and leather mask. But the pink tutu and satin bustier his friend had also been wearing were another matter altogether, not to mention the feather whip. Brady wished for about the hundredth time this morning that the commissioner wasn't in bed with the flu. He should be here holding Henley's hand so Brady could get back to solving the city's latest murder.

A minute passed, then another. Brady sighed, then spoke quietly but directly. "Sir, I did what I could to squash the media coverage. But Sanderson was very well known, and..." He stopped, knowing he didn't have to tell the mayor how bad this was going to look when it hit the papers. And it would hit the papers. Morton Sanderson was a major player in the Philadelphia business community and a chief backer of Henley's upcoming reelection campaign. He was also a self-righteous blowhard, notorious for his public drubbing of anyone who fell short of his strict code of morality.

Which made that pink tutu particularly hard to deal with.

"Well, I don't think you or anyone else is going to be able to make this go away or keep it under wraps," Brady finished. He hated all this political-posturing crap. He wasn't good at pussyfooting around, much less putting positive spins on things that weren't remotely positive. He'd gotten where he was by focusing on one thing and one thing only: getting to the truth. He stood straighter. "To be frank, sir, I need to get back to the station. I've got interviews lined up all morning and I can't afford to waste time on who is going to write what in the morning papers."

The mayor swung back around, appearing ready to blast him for his insubordination, but abruptly stopped. His expression turned weary, but it was the real grief in the depths of his eyes that made Brady rein in his impatience.

"Just find out who set him up, O'Keefe," Henley said quietly. "I'll take care of the media."

"Sir, with respect, there is no indication of a setup. Not yet anyway."

"I know Mort rubbed a lot of people the wrong way, but I know—knew—him better than most. No way did he die in a seedy hotel while taking part in some sort of kinky sex scandal. There's something else going on here. Find the truth, Detective O'Keefe. And find it fast."

"Yes, sir."

Henley was already on the phone before Brady hit the door. Once in the hall, he added under his breath, "But whether or not you like the truth is not my problem."

BRADY SLUGGED DOWN the foul dregs of a cold mug of coffee. When he didn't even wince, he knew it was time to call it quits for the night. He slapped shut the folder he'd been writing in and shoved back his chair. "I'm out of here," he said to no one in particular. His shift had left hours ago and the midnight shift was already busily at work, not paying him any particular mind. Which was why he worked late more often than not. No one bugged him, his phone didn't ring and he got a lot done. Besides, when he was on a case, there was nothing else he'd rather be doing. And in this city, there was always a case.

"Detective O'Keefe still around?"

Brady swung his head toward the squad room door. "Who wants to know?"

Sergeant Ross wove through the desks toward him. "Some woman named Mahoney, out in receiving. Says the mayor sent her."

"I didn't get a call from Henley's office." Even as he completed the sentence he dug under the folders on his desk to the stack of pink message slips the secretary had stuck in his hand the last time he came in. He'd been so besieged, he'd never gotten to them. Henley's message was the sixth one down. He swore under his breath. "Yeah, all right. Tell her I'll be out in a minute."

He shrugged on his suit jacket, but didn't bother putting on his tie. It was late, he was wiped out and hungry and suddenly wishing he'd left with the rest of his squad. He scanned the message slip again. Erin Mahoney. He smiled wryly. Boy did that name bring back memories. None good. He'd known an Erin Mahoney growing up. She was two years younger than him, but she'd made his life hell right up until the last day of fourth grade when she'd blessedly moved across town.

He spent a moment wondering whatever happened to her, then chuckled. Probably torturing some poor insurance salesman husband and wreaking havoc with the PTA. The image made Brady feel better. He only had to deal with murderers and reluctant witnesses. And whatever flunky Mayor Henley had just shoved in his path.

Still smiling, he pushed through the door, then stopped in his tracks. Her back was to him...and what a back it was. Tall and shapely, with deep auburn hair, she wore a suit so beautifully tailored it almost made him wish he'd taken up Uncle Mike's offer to work at his clothing store instead of entering the police academy eleven years ago. Never before had a tape measure held such erotic possibilities.

His appreciative smile froze when she stopped chatting up the desk clerk and swung around to face him.

"Terror Mahoney." He'd said it under his breath, but the mischievous light that twinkled in her bright green eyes signaled that she'd heard him.

"Why if it isn't Crybaby O'Keefe." She laughed when he scowled. She turned back to the very attentive desk sergeant. "Thank you, Sergeant Ross," she said, then bent gracefully and snapped up her briefcase. Despite his dumbfounded state, or maybe because of it, he followed her movement, causing him to reflect on just how much finer a pair of basic black high heels could make prizewinning legs appear.

She walked by Brady in those basic black pumps and opened the door he'd just come through. "Is there somewhere we can talk?"

Her bright smile and knowing look made it clear she knew exactly where he'd been looking, and that she'd absolutely planned it that way. It was as if the intervening twenty years had never happened. She'd been in his face for less than a minute and she already had him on the defensive. Her weapons had changed a bit—okay, a lot—but they were still just as effective.

Well, he told himself, he was no longer a skinny little ten-year-old. Nor did he adhere to the code of honor that said a man didn't stand tough against a woman. The first time a woman had pulled a gun on him had ended that notion. Erin's weapon of choice had always been her mouth.

"I don't suppose it would do any good to ask you to postpone this little chat until tomorrow?" he said. "I was off duty about—" he glanced at his watch "—yesterday."

"I know it's late, but I've been in meetings with the mayor all day. Henley is expecting me in his office first thing in the morning. I need to talk with you before then. I know Henley left a message with you."

Resigned, Brady sighed, and motioned her toward his desk. "Over there, second desk on your right."

She turned around, causing him to stop short. "Is there somewhere a bit more private? This is...delicate."

She smelled good. Damn good. No delicate little floral scent for Terror Mahoney. No, she ambushed men right up front with something spicy and cinnamon sweet. Of course, anything would smell good to him after fourteen hours of bad coffee. Or so he told himself. "You're here about the Sanderson murder, right?"

"Yes. Can we use an interview room or something?"

"Everyone here knows the details, Ms. Mahoney."

"First I'm Terror, now I'm a Ms.?"

He found a smile even if he did have to grit his teeth to form it. "When I saw you I remembered you as an eight-year-old pain in the ass. Now I see you're going to be a twenty-eight-year-old pain in the ass. But I've matured." He swept a hand in front of him. "Have a seat, madam?"

She didn't scowl. In fact, she laughed and looked him over. "Yes, you have matured." Her gaze traveled up his chest and over his face. "Quite well, I must say." She smiled. "And it's *Miss.*"

He swore he felt that look ripple over every bristle of his five o'clock shadow. Damn, he was more exhausted than he realized. Brady thought he had done an admirable job of not noticing she'd also matured quite well. Of course he'd noticed, only a dead man wouldn't have noticed. But at least he hadn't been obvious about it. "You didn't turn out so bad either," he managed to say.

She laughed again. "Boy, how much did that hurt?" She didn't wait for an answer. Instead she folded her long frame into the metal chair. She crossed one leg over the other, and it would have taken a far better man than him not to be aware that her legs truly did go on forever.

He'd always thought he was that better man. He didn't thank her for proving otherwise. He tore his gaze away from the forest-green suit she was wearing, trying hard not to think about how it seemed to have been stitched directly onto her body. He usually gave less than a damn about his suits or how they fit, but she made him feel exceedingly rumpled. One more point against her.

He rubbed a hand across the back of his neck, ignoring that he was long overdue for a haircut, and sat behind his desk. He was hip deep in the city's most sensational murder investigation in years. The last thing he had time for was the testosterone tango. And he had less than no time to play with someone like Erin Mahoney. She'd obviously spent the last twenty years honing her warrior skills to dangerously new, and exceedingly feminine, heights.

"So, what does the mayor want to know?" he asked. Business, this was going to be all business. Short, not-too-sweet, and over. "And since when are you working for him?"

"He wants to know exactly what you know about

who killed Morton Sanderson and why. And since about nine-fifteen this morning when he hired my firm to help him out with his little...media concern.''

"Firm? You have a firm?"

"You're not the only one who grew up and got a responsible job, O'Keefe. I'm in public relations. Mahoney and Briggs. Perhaps you've heard of us?"

Public relations? Terror Mahoney? He'd have laughed, except one look at her expression told him she was waiting for exactly that. So he shrugged. "Sorry, no, I haven't."

She shrugged as well, not remotely offended. "We're small, but we have a solid reputation."

"What is it, exactly, that you do?"

"I'm a consultant. People hire me for all kinds of reasons. Self-promotion, business promotion, media liaison—"

"Ah. A spin doctor."

Her smooth expression didn't falter. "In this case, it's my job to make sure said media doesn't turn this thing with Sanderson into some kind of salacious, kinky-sex droolathon." At his look of disbelief, she amended, "Okay, more than they already have." She lifted a hand. "I'm not here to make your life difficult."

Now he had to laugh. "At no time in our mutual past history have you done anything but make my life as difficult as possible. The only change I see now is that you're getting paid to do it." He folded his arms and leaned back in his chair. "Nice work if you can get it."

"It is nice work," she retorted with a smile. "And I get paid quite well, thank you." She shifted in her seat and he worked damn hard to keep his gaze squarely on her face. "And because I get paid quite well, I take that job very seriously," she went on. "I won't be a disruption as long as you keep an open line of communication with me. All you have to do is report to me everything you discover, as you discover it, so I can prepare all public statements that come from both this precinct and the mayor's office. No one is to talk to any member of the press unless they clear it with me first."

"Says who?"

"Says me. With the mayor's blessing, of course."

"Well, you'll have to talk with the commissioner."

"I believe the mayor has already done that."

Brady swore under his breath. Commissioner Douglas had been appointed by Henley, and with the mayor up for reelection, that meant Douglas had become his number-one patsy. To hell with what was right or wrong, it was all about job security now.

"Consider me your liaison." She recrossed her legs. "If you think about it, O'Keefe, I'm actually here to make your life easier. You won't have to deal with the press at all. You'll only have to deal with me."

Brady simply stared at her. She was truly amazing. And insane if she thought he was going to go along with this plan like a good little boy. "I never thought I could be given a set of choices that would make me think dealing directly with the press was the preferable option."

Nothing seemed to faze her. Her smile was honest and direct. "Don't make it sound so bad, Detective. I'm sure we'll make this work with a minimum of fuss."

"You are truly an optimist then." He shoved back his chair and stood.

For the first time, she looked a bit off balance. Good. He'd have to remember how he did that. He had a feeling he'd need to use it. Repeatedly.

"Wait a minute, I need to go over your reports so far." There was a touch of nervousness in her voice now as she watched him clear his desk.

"I need to go home and get some sleep." He scooped up the case files and piled them into a side drawer, then locked it. He dropped the keys in his shirt pocket, pausing by her chair as he rounded the desk. "And if you plan to accompany me to bed in hopes I talk in my sleep, I'll save you the effort."

"But—"

"Good night, Ms. Mahoney. Tell Mayor Henley that I'll file my report with my captain as soon as I'm ready. Until then, he can contact Commissioner Douglas if he has any questions about the investigation." Brady decided he'd rather deal with them directly than go through her anyway. And he was certain that confrontation would come sooner rather than later. But it wasn't right now, and that was all he cared about at the moment.

He lifted a finger when she opened her mouth to speak. "As for the press, don't worry. As a rule, I don't talk to anyone about any of my cases. Ever." His pointed look at her was clearly understood.

He was halfway across the room when he realized she wasn't dogging his heels as he'd expected. At no time had Terror Mahoney ever given up easily. So he stopped and turned back. His grin widened. She didn't disappoint. She was looking at the tag board where the officers hung keys to the squad cars when not in use, only she wouldn't know what those keys were for.

"Mahoney," he called out, causing her to swing around. He had to give it to her, she managed to look totally innocent. About as innocent as a barracuda in a school of guppies, he thought, but there was no resentment in it. Quite the opposite actually. But then, he was no guppy. He patted his pocket. "I've got the only set." He saluted her. "Good night."

With a rueful smile, she saluted him back.

He left the squad room feeling her eyes on his back. All up and down his back for that matter. His neck grew red, but he found himself smiling as he walked out to his car.

2

ERIN MAHONEY WATCHED with more than a little appreciation as Brady O'Keefe strolled across the street toward city hall. He looked good. Better than good, she amended as he drew closer, noticing he'd shaved.

Until he'd walked through that door last night, she'd had no idea Brady worked for the police department. In fact, she hadn't even thought of him in years. But the surprise had been a pleasant one. She was fairly certain Brady did not share that sentiment.

Of course, thinking back, he had every reason to be wary. She'd been a real handful as a child. She'd come from a large family, middle child of seven, so her parents hadn't paid strict attention to her. Heck, they'd hardly paid any attention to her. Which had suited her fine at the time. She'd gotten plenty of attention—both wanted and unwanted—from her six brothers. And she'd managed to grow up and be a responsible adult despite it all.

She supposed she should have known Brady would end up a detective. He came from a long line of cops. She knew his dad and granddad had been on the Philly force, as had an uncle. She thought again about the meeting she'd just left with the mayor and commissioner—the latter, still in bed with the flu, attending by phone conference. They'd sung Brady's praises to the moon, regaling her with stories of the amazing feats of detective work that had led him to be one of the top-ranked detectives on the force. Pretty impressive for someone who'd just hit thirty.

They'd also made it clear, though she'd already come to the same conclusion, that he wouldn't take lightly to their plan. However, they hadn't backed down on it either. A lot was riding on making this situation go away quickly and quietly. They told her they expected her to live up to her own not-so-humble reputation and get the job done. Whatever it took.

And she'd decided what it took was for her and Brady to have a meeting when both of them were rested and thinking clearly. Hence her planned ambush on the steps today.

She watched as he dodged a turning car and rounded the back of a double-parked taxi. Good reflexes. For a scrawny kid, he'd sure...filled out. So much for thinking clearly, she thought with a laugh. But the man did make her hormones jump, there was no denying that. Of course, she was pretty sure that wasn't one-sided. Not that she'd ever condoned using sex as a means to get the job done. Well, not directly anyway. Sex and sexuality were two distinctly different things. She never used the former, but she was acutely aware how to effectively use the latter.

Women had few enough weapons in the high-stakes world of career-building. She was a firm believer in using every one she had to its fullest potential.

The mayor had said "whatever it takes," she mused,

still watching him approach...and found the hard line she drew between sexuality and sex blurring just a teensy bit.

"Good morning."

He looked more resigned than surprised to see her. "Morning," he said. "I'm withholding judgment on the good part."

"I need to talk to you."

"Judgment withheld permanently."

She couldn't help noticing that his voice was as rough this morning as it had been last night. Was it always that way? She shook that thought loose immediately. She'd really have to make a serious effort not to get so distracted here. This was business, not pleasure. Damn shame, that.

"Come on, I'm not so bad, am I?" she asked, unable to resist teasing him. Just a little.

He looked at her briefcase, then back up at her. There was the tiniest glint of teasing in his own incredible blue eyes. "Depends on what you have in there."

She laughed now. "I assure you, I outgrew playing silly pranks a long time ago."

"Yeah, well, I've always been one to believe things when I have concrete proof. Never go on hearsay. Gets you into trouble every time."

"Not a bad motto, Detective." *Work, Erin, no more flirting.* But that tiny glint was just too damn tempting. And this wasn't really flirting. More like baiting. Twenty years later and she still couldn't resist yanking his chain a little.

She grinned and held her arms wide. "Wanna frisk me?"

His eyes registered surprise, but only for a brief second, noticeable only because she'd been looking for it. So he wasn't easy to knock off balance, she admitted. Not at age ten...and most certainly not now. Probably why it had always been so irresistible to try.

"I don't frisk. I get search warrants," he responded evenly. But again, there was that trace, that tiny little trace of appreciation in his expression that egged her on.

She dropped her arms to her side. "Killjoy."

"I guess you'll just have to hunt for other game today, Ms. Mahoney." He nodded, then went to move past her. She reached out and held his arm, stopping him. He looked down at her from the step above.

Bad tactical error, she acknowledged immediately. She made a mental note of it, but had no idea where it got filed because he chose that moment to smile at her. A real smile.

"I'm not going to discuss the case, Erin. Not now. Not later. Not until after I've finished my investigation."

She released his arm, but stepped up so they were on even ground. It didn't give her much of an edge, she realized. Barely a sliver, in fact. His smile was gone, but only from his mouth. It was still there, all smug and male, in his eyes.

"You on your way in to see the mayor?" she asked, a touch of smugness in her own voice.

"I am." The twinkle died. "Why?"

A hollow victory, she discovered. She liked the twinkle better, as it turned out. *Eye on the prize, Erin, not his*— "I'll escort you in, then," she said quickly.

"That's not necessary," he said.

She slid her arm though his and propelled him up the stairs before he knew what she was up to. Keep the opposition off balance she reminded herself, before they could do the same to you. "Well, I might as well walk you up, since I'll be joining you." She gave him a megawatt smile, then slid her arm free and pushed open the lobby door. "After you?"

He looked at her, then simply nodded and walked through. "Thank you." Being the gentleman, he opened the inner door for her. "After you." His seemingly benign smile, on closer inspection as she passed by, was actually a shade on the insolent side.

Rather than feel deflated, she felt...energized. She was also incredibly turned on, but that was a very unprofessional reaction, so she tried hard to ignore it. Crybaby O'Keefe? Making her hot?

Okay, she told herself as they headed to the mayor's office. Playtime was most definitely over. She switched mental gears and worked on coming up with a quick game plan on how to handle the meeting. A meeting she hadn't been invited to. But she was sure the mayor wasn't going to throw her out. She merely had to engineer the thing from the start to go the way she wanted it to. She had no compunction in working the mayor to suit her own needs, even though he was her client. After all, as long as the outcome was what he'd hired her to accomplish, that was what was most important, right?

She caught a glimpse of Brady's face as the receptionist led them back to Henley's office. He looked as if he was going to war. And perhaps he wasn't far off.

Going through the mayor to get Brady to do what she wanted—needed—him to do was really the only way. And it would tick him off. Big time. But maybe that was for the best, too. All this hormonal stuff sparking between them could only be a bad thing.

Really bad. Because it felt too damn good.

She used the moment Brady turned to close the door behind them to make her first defensive strike. His loss for always being a gentleman she told herself as she charged into battle.

BRADY CLOSED the door and turned to find Erin striding confidently across the expanse of carpet to intercept Henley before he could take charge of the meeting. Very effective, he thought, silently applauding the maneuver. He'd used the same one many times. Only he usually didn't enter smiling. Or moving his hips like that.

She blocked his view of Henley, but he got the distinct impression the mayor wasn't expecting them both. Hmm. So, the question was, had she been waiting for him to show up and use him as her entrée? Or had she just come out of the building and spied him on his way in? He bet on the latter.

He smiled. She'd probably gotten her battle plan in place with the mayor and thought it was her lucky day when she'd snagged him on his way in. Only he hadn't succumbed to the sex-charged fog she'd effortlessly swirled around the two of them and answered all her questions without a fight. But she hadn't pouted and given up, she'd merely switched tactics.

He liked that in an opponent.

The fact that there were still some remnants of that fog swirling around inside him was probably the reason he was being so damn reasonable about the whole thing. Well, that and the fact that pretty much nothing was going to make him change his mind about dealing with her on this investigation. Nothing short of the commissioner himself, ordering him to—

"Detective O'Keefe? Please have a seat. I have a phone conference ready to go with Commissioner Douglas."

Brady kept his gaze averted from Erin and made certain the litany of curses running through his mind were not reflected in his expression. It wasn't easy.

He sat in a purposefully relaxed manner. "Good morning, Mayor. Commissioner Douglas."

"O'Keefe?" The commissioner's scratchy voice rasped through the speakerphone.

"Yes, sir?"

"I want an update on my desk by noon. It will be couriered to me. In the meantime, I want you to stop giving Ms. Mahoney such a hard time here and work with her. I don't expect you to compromise the investigation, but we have a press conference this afternoon and we need a concrete plan on how we're going to handle this with the media. I don't have to spell out for you the sensitive nature of this matter. Mayor Henley is grieving the loss of one of his dearest friends and—"

And the loss of almost five percent on the overnight polls, Brady added mentally, striving to hold on to his temper.

"The community is shaken up over the whole sordid ordeal. I know how involved this case is, which is why I brought Erin in in the first place. She will free all of us up to do our jobs and from having to deal with the press."

"With all due respect," Brady began, still not looking at Erin, "you've always allowed me to handle my investigations the way I see fit. And I don't think allowing a civilian to be privy to the innermost details of a homicide investigation, especially this one, is a positive move." He held up his hand when Erin tried to interrupt. "Furthermore, I've never had a problem handling the press and I don't expect this case will be any different."

The mayor cleared his throat. "Detective O'Keefe, no one is challenging the way you handle your investigation, but I think you'll agree that, in the past, the relationship between you and the media has been somewhat...strained."

"What he's trying to say, O'Keefe," the commissioner broke in, "is that you're a stubborn pain in the ass and you don't give a good goddamn what the media thinks of how you run things."

Erin choked on a chuckle and Brady couldn't ignore it. So he did the last thing she'd expect, he winked at her. The resulting flash of shock on her face was very satisfying. He turned back to the speakerphone and the mayor, who had missed the little exchange. "Very true, Commissioner," he said. "So I don't see why we should change what has always been an effective policy to date. I tell them nothing, they stew and dig harder, I tell them nothing, they fill their columns with wild speculation and false leads, then I solve the crime, it all comes out in the wash and we go on to the next public debacle."

Erin crossed her legs the other way, costing him a split second in timing, but a crucial one as it gave her the opening she'd been waiting for. "Gentlemen, if I might intrude." She turned that polished PR smile on him. He hated it, which for some strange reason, made him smile in return. That made her blink, even if only for a second.

Damn, but this was kind of fun. Fun in a very this-can't-be-good-for-me way.

"Detective O'Keefe," she said, the smile toned down now. Point for Brady. "I understand how pointless this may seem to you, but even you must admit that in an election year, something like this case can have far reaching consequences. This is no longer simply about solving a murder. It's about protecting innocent people's reputations and possibly their livelihoods." She relaxed and exuded that "everything will be fine if you simply trust me" vibe. "I don't have to know every gritty detail. I merely need a brief conference with you on how I want to handle this with the press. All I need from you are enough details to support my angle."

"Your *angle?*"

Brady looked to the mayor, who had been watching them like someone at a tennis match. Henley seemed more than happy to allow Erin to handle things and didn't use the moment to jump to Brady's defense. Coward, Brady thought.

"There is a way to present the situation to the public," she continued insistently, "even to feed their need for titillation, without compromising the innocent."

Brady had to hide his smile when her last comment got a visible reaction from the mayor.

"Now, Ms. Mahoney," he blustered, finally looking a little concerned, "I really don't think—"

The confident smile returned. "Mayor Henley, we've been over this." She leaned forward, oozing sincerity. "I know exactly what line to walk and how not to cross it."

And Henley totally bought it. Brady swore under his breath, knowing he'd just lost this hand.

To her credit, she didn't gloat. She turned to him and flipped open her Palm Pilot. With total businesslike mien, she looked at the small screen. "I can give you thirty minutes right now," she said. As if he were the one demanding her time. Very clever.

Brady knew when to hold and when to fold. He also knew a new hand got dealt each round. So she'd won this one...it wasn't as if she'd made a run on the house. Not yet, anyway.

He turned smoothly toward the mayor. "Can we use your conference room?"

The mayor didn't bother to hide his relief. His mood was now as expansive as his smile. "By all means." He waved them inside the long room that connected with his office. "I'll have Teri come in with some coffee."

"Thank you," they said in unison.

Brady waited until the mayor's secretary had come and gone, then took his time pouring his coffee. He even fixed Erin a mug. "Sugar?"

She eyed him warily now. "Black is fine."

He slid the mug toward her and took a seat catty-corner to her at one end of the immense black table. With a relaxed smile that gave away none of what he was really feeling, he asked, "So, what is your angle?"

She leaned forward and pushed her mug aside. Folding her arms on the table, she looked him right in the eye. "Why don't you tell me yours first?"

3

ERIN STUDIED Brady closely, but couldn't tell what was going on behind those enigmatic eyes of his.

He shrugged, looking for all the world as if he couldn't care less that the commissioner and mayor had basically just sold him down the river. "I don't have an angle."

"So just like that you're going to give me everything I want?" *Careful, Erin.* Those eyes had flared, even if only a tiny fraction. At any other time she'd have jumped on that zap of electrical energy that had just shot between them. She would have worked it right up to the edge of professional acceptability. Meaning just enough to reduce her opponent to a quivering mass of hormones, but far shy of allowing him to believe it would ever lead to anything. Much less anything serious.

Now, fun and casual? *That* she might be up for. Just not with Brady. There was nothing fun or casual about Brady O'Keefe. Dangerous and unpredictable, that was Brady. She'd never encountered electricity of the type that seemed to flare up every time she came within ten feet of him.

But she didn't lean back now. Because her job demanded she didn't. And as long as she remembered she was here on a job, one that could push her small firm into the spotlight, she'd be fine.

When Brady didn't respond to her challenge, she opted to take control of the meeting. Something she should have done last night. She cleared her throat and got to work. "I want to present this as a homicide. The brutal slaying of a well-known member of Philadelphia's upper crust. We will focus on Sanderson's numerous philanthropic contributions and what a loss his death will be to the underprivileged. We want to stir up outrage that such a worthy member of society has been taken from us. We want people demanding this obviously deranged killer be caught."

"Erin—"

She talked over him. "I'm well aware that the media's focus is going to be on the kinky sexual elements present at the scene of the murder." She stopped and looked at him. "You have ruled this a homicide, am I correct?"

Brady stared at her for such a prolonged moment, she was certain he was going to balk, or get up and walk out. In the end, he did neither. But there was no electricity now. She wasn't exactly relieved. Not a good sign.

"We'll have the full report from the medical examiner later today," he said finally. "But preliminary findings are edging toward heart attack." He leaned back, but didn't go so far as to smile smugly. Though she sensed he wanted to. "Not exactly the brutal slaying you are so anxious to depict."

"So, he what then? Died of an overdose of sex? I mean, this is a murder investigation, isn't it?"

"Right now we're waiting to hear the final postmortem from Theo. Until then we treat it as a homicide. Once the results are in, we'll rule whether there was foul play." He looked her in the eye. "Or whether ol' Morty preached hard-line morality to the people, while privately practicing something fairly...well, amoral, certainly by his own standards anyway." He folded his arms. "You have an angle on how to play that possibility to the media?"

She swallowed a curse word and didn't much like the taste. "Brady, if Sanderson is portrayed as some kind of sex pervert, there will be total chaos in the mayor's political party while everyone tries to run and distance themselves from the guy. I've already got Henley's campaign manager breathing down my neck over this."

Brady shrugged. "Not really my problem. My problem is to determine if Morty died getting his satin-covered rocks off, or if someone helped him along a bit. But I'm here to tell you, your job isn't going to be easy either way. Morty was not well liked. There are people who will come out of the woodwork to crucify him when they get wind of this."

"Exactly," Erin retorted. "Chaos. And with the mayor being a close friend of Morton's, this could blow up in everyone's face. It would destroy his campaign. The mudslinging will make everyone look bad."

"So basically you don't care what really happened. You just want the mayor to come out looking good for reelection. That is what he's paying you the big bucks for, right?"

She didn't take offense. This was part of the job, too. Though not her favorite part. "What I care about is successfully getting my client through a rough personal spot with the least amount of personal and professional damage I can manage. That is why he hired me. And honestly, I didn't think taking on a job for the mayor was exactly something to be ashamed of."

"You don't care about the truth then? Just the most positive spin you can put on it."

Erin blew out a breath and tried to clamp down on her rapidly growing frustration. Why she cared what Brady thought of her was beyond her. He was supposed to be a means to an end. But his words had stung, there was no denying that. "Look at it this way. I'm like an attorney who has to occasionally represent a guilty person and still do her utmost to get him the best deal within the bounds of the law. I occasionally work for someone who is caught in a less than ideal position and do my darnedest to lessen the negative impact."

"For the record, I think most attorneys are slimeballs, no matter who they are representing."

Now she smiled. It was that or throw something at him. "So I'm a slimeball?"

"No, you're a professional spin doctor who just might have jumped in over her head into shark-infested political waters where people play for keeps. This isn't about prettying up some businessman's brush with a drug bust."

She smacked the table. "Okay, now you're really ticking me off. I don't really give a flying hot damn what you think of me, the mayor, or even Mort Sanderson. Finding out how Sanderson died and who might have killed him is not my job. Someone else has to worry about that, namely you. My only interest is seeing that this whole thing doesn't drag my client through the sewage Ol' Morty might have been wallowing in. How I present things to the media is strictly meant to help him, not hinder you. So there is absolutely no reason why you can't continue your fight for truth and justice, while I protect the people who are getting caught in the crossfire."

"So, if what I discover ends up painting the mayor in a less than positive light, you'll just spin that the right way too, whether or not he might be a slimeball as well?"

Righteous indignation fled as a frown instantly creased her forehead. "Do you have any indication Henley is in any way involved in this? Personally?"

Brady laughed. "You're a piece of work, you know that? But I can see why you're doing so well. You do keep your eye on the end goal, no matter what blows across your path." He pushed back his chair. "Your thirty minutes are up."

"I want you to let me know the instant you get the report back. I'm going to push the press conference back to four-thirty."

"Wouldn't want to miss that five o'clock newscast."

"No," she said, looking him straight in the eye. "*We* wouldn't. But if this isn't a murder, I need to know.

Otherwise I'm going with what I told you earlier. We need to steer this thing away from how he was found and toward catching the psycho that killed him. I would think you'd want that, too."

"If there is a psycho killer."

She stood and blocked his path. "Last I heard, the press only knew that he'd been found in the Dew Lily Inn and that there was supposition that his reason for being there was sexual."

"No one is at the Dew Lily Inn unless it's sexual."

"Point taken. But the rest has been kept under wraps, right?"

"There are strict orders on those who were at the scene. Until I finish my interviews, it's in the best interest of the investigation—not to mention your job—to keep the rest sealed. Now, how long that will last, I can't say. You know how this town is."

"You've talked to people, conducted some interviews already. What do you think happened?"

"I think I don't make guesses. Now excuse me. I have to get back to work."

That he felt his work was more important than hers came through loud and clear. "I'll expect a call from you," she said, "or I'll be camped out at the precinct until I get an answer."

He turned back at the door. "You know where my desk is." Then he left.

She turned to the table, hands clenched, working hard not to toss her mug across the room. She was normally not a violent woman, but Brady... The man was impossible! Couldn't he see she was just trying to do her job, here? She wasn't deliberately doing anything to get in his way, nor was she hurting anyone. If anything, she was keeping the press off his back and putting them squarely onto hers. "He should be thanking me, dammit."

She downed the rest of her coffee, knowing it would likely be all she had until dinner, then snapped her briefcase shut and headed out the door. She had a lot of work to get done before the press conference. Not the least of which was figuring out how in the hell she was going to spin this if Sanderson had in fact just died of a heart attack while playing kinky sex games.

BRADY WAS surprised when he returned from the morgue and did not spy a certain long-legged redhead perched at his desk. He spun a wary glance around the squad room. Nope, he was in the clear. He walked to his desk, totally ignoring the sense of disappointment he'd felt. And it was not smug disappointment either. Theo hadn't been able to rule out foul play. It had been a heart attack, but there didn't seem to be anything to back up why it had happened to an otherwise healthy forty-nine-year-old man. There had also been no sexual activity. They were running toxicology tests to see if anything had been introduced to his system to induce heart failure.

Until then, Brady had to keep working the case as a homicide. And Erin got to continue with her spin doctoring.

He wasn't exactly sure what ticked him off so badly about it all. He'd had plenty of time to think it over while waiting for the overworked medical examiner. She was right about getting the press off his back. She was even right about playing down the sexual nature of the scene where Mort had been found. And he wasn't so naive as to believe that any politician worth his constituents' votes was going to let something of this caliber careen wildly down the media tracks without doing his or her damnedest to steer the train. Or hire someone who could steer the train. That someone being Erin Mahoney.

He had to grudgingly admit that she also seemed pretty damn good at her job.

He just wished like hell her job hadn't crossed paths with his. He might admire her professional acumen, but that didn't mean he trusted her. She'd made no bones about the fact that her loyalty was vested solely in saving Henley's political ass. If she had to climb all over Brady and his investigation to do it, he had no doubt she would. He did not like anyone breathing down his neck.

The scent of her perfume wafted through his mind. Along with images of her climbing all over him and breathing down his neck...literally. He groaned and once again shoved the thought away. Erin was dangerous enough without giving her that sort of leverage. Even in the privacy of his own, suddenly feverish, mind.

The sound of a throat clearing just behind him brought him around. So the perfume had been real. He should have known. He could only thank God she had no way of knowing what thoughts—and images—had just been playing though his head.

"You're late," he said, taking the offensive. He'd already learned it didn't pay to let her have the upper hand. Not even for a second.

"I do have other things to do besides dog your every move. Besides, I knew where to find you when I was ready." She smiled. "You look a little let down, though. Who'd have guessed?"

She was just razzing him. No way did his expression reveal anything. And he hadn't been let down, dammit.

When he didn't respond, her smile faded and she was all business again.

"You got the report from the medical examiner? I've got—" she glanced at the slim gold watch circling her wrist "—twenty minutes to show time." She looked him right in the eye. "So what angle am I playing?"

Brady really hated being party to her part in all this. He was tempted to just shove the file at her and let her come to her own damn conclusions and spin the press conference any way she saw fit. But technically anything said or done that dealt in any way with this case fell under his jurisdiction and it would be sloppy of him not to watch every move she made like a hawk.

"No conclusive evidence," he said, not bothering to deflect the matter either. If he was going to have to deal with her—and it was apparent after this morning that he had zero choice there—he wasn't going to waste more time than absolutely necessary on it. He raised a hand when she would have interrupted. He would be in charge, however. Whether she liked it or not. "There are enough unusual elements that we can't rule out foul play. He did die of a heart attack."

Her mouth dropped open in dismay.

"But we're running toxicology tests to see if he wasn't helped along there a bit." She snapped her mouth shut, not entirely happy with the circumstances, but apparently knowing better than to badger him about it. Because she didn't, he found himself opening his mouth and giving her another small bit. "There was no evidence of any semen."

Now her eyebrows lifted. "Really?"

He had to smile. "What, you really didn't believe your own angle? This is good news for your side, you know."

"Since when are you concerned about my side?" She smiled, but waved a hand before he could reply. "Forget that. I should be thanking you for giving me the information without making me wheedle it out of you."

"For the record, I don't respond well to wheedling."

"So I've noticed." They stood there, staring at each other several moments longer than necessary. Just as the tension between them turned...questionable, she turned and nodded to the file on his desk. "Is that the report?"

"Don't push it, Mahoney. I've already given you more than I have to. Just make sure you don't hurt the investigation with it."

"I don't know whether to be offended or complimented. But don't worry, your trust hasn't been misplaced."

"Who said anything about trust?" He moved behind his desk. For some reason, simply standing near her made his body hum. The width of the desk wasn't much of a barrier, but he'd take what he could get. "For the time being, our goals are falling on a somewhat mutual plane. I have to do more digging now, and keeping the press off the sexual angle works for me."

"So you're saying you think this was a murder? And Sanderson was set up to be found like that?"

He looked directly at her. "*I'm* not saying anything."

She sighed. "Will you be at the press conference?"

"You seem to have that covered. I don't need to be answering questions that are better left unasked until I have more information." He pulled his chair out, signaling that their meeting was over.

Erin jotted a few notes on a notepad, then slid it back in the satchel she had slung over her shoulder. "Thanks, Brady."

"Don't thank me. You're the one that has to deal with the wolves this afternoon."

"Why is it I think you're starting to like this division of labor?"

"Did I say that?" *How did she do that?* He'd been all business, then she pulled a smile out of him with seemingly little effort.

"I'm beginning to realize it's what you don't say that a woman should pay attention to."

"I beg your pardon?"

She laughed. "That's one thing that hasn't changed about you, Brady. I could never make you beg for anything.'' She turned and he knew he'd been sucked in too deep, because he watched her move and angle that shapely body of hers past each and every desk on her way to the door.

She turned at the door, catching him watching her. "I'll call you when the conference is over and give you an update."

He could only nod. When she was gone, he sat down heavily in his chair. He closed his eyes, but he could still see her face, the sharp intelligence fairly glowing in those green eyes of hers, the delighted little twinkle that surfaced when she teased him. She might be a knockout, but it was the self-assurance she wore, as perfectly tailored as those hot little suits she shrugged into each morning, that was the more potent aphrodisiac.

Make him beg? Oh yes. She'd been back in his life less than twenty-four hours and he already wanted to beg her for mercy. But mercy in what form?

4

ERIN STRODE into her office and dropped her briefcase onto her desk with a thump. She dropped into her chair with similar enthusiasm.

Her business partner and best friend, Gina Briggs, walked in a second later. She was as short as Erin was tall, but no less bold. She had thick, dark hair worn short and spiky around her face, her eyes were a vivid blue and her mouth was wide and expressive. Mainly because it was usually moving. Today was no different.

"I'm sorry, I missed the news. I was tied up trying to get Tony out of a fix with the news director." Tony Hallman was a popular local anchorman who had recently hired Mahoney and Briggs to beef up his public profile in hopes of getting a bump to a bigger market. Women loved him and his ratings were good. Unfortunately, women loved him because he was gorgeous and had a sexy deep voice, not because he was a particularly good journalist.

Erin groaned, glad to have something to think about besides the disastrous press conference she'd just hosted. "Don't tell me. He ad-libbed his own questions again?"

Gina nodded. "He thinks he's showing his ability to

be flexible and hard-hitting," she said with a sigh. "But he comes off looking like a moron. Ever since he heard he was up for the possible pickup in New York he's been an egotistical nightmare."

Erin raised an eyebrow. "Like he wasn't before?"

Gina laughed easily. "Oh, his ego has always been healthy. But he controlled it, understood his strengths."

"Yeah, big white teeth and a voice that would melt chocolate."

"Exactly. Now he thinks he's Tom freaking Brokaw. If he doesn't watch out, not only will he lose his New York slot, but he'll be looking for a new market outside Philly as well. Today his news director hit the roof, and chewed out Tony big time." She shook her head. "What is it with men?"

Erin must have given away her own current view on the opposite sex because Gina instantly forgot all about Tony and perched attentively on the edge of the desk. "So, was Detective Hunk at the press conference?"

Erin glared at Gina, who was entirely unrepentant.

"Hey, I've checked him out." Gina shook a hand in front of her. "Talk about melting chocolate. I say we should work with Philly's finest more often. And I do mean finest."

"Enough already." But there was little heat in Erin's rebuke. She'd known Gina since their first day of college, and because they'd shared everything ever since, she'd already let it slip that Brady O'Keefe was flying in under her hormone radar way too often for her peace of mind. Let alone her peace of body.

Gina tapped a pen on Erin's desk. "I don't see any reason, when this isn't all over, why you two shouldn't just burn each other out of your respective systems."

"What I need is help getting through right now. I can't worry about after." She let her head sink to her desk. "Of course, that might not be a problem after the mayor fires me."

Gina tugged at Erin's arm. "What?" She hopped off the desk. "Now Tony really owes me. I can't believe I missed this. What happened? You had this totally under control. Did the hunk ruin it? I know you said he wasn't thrilled you were his media mouthpiece, but he wouldn't intentionally jeopardize—"

Erin held up a hand to halt the onslaught. "I don't know that Brady was even there."

Gina's eyes twinkled. "Brady, huh." She motioned with her hands. "Go on, just commenting here. Continue."

Erin leaned back in her chair. "I need coffee. And aspirin. And a shot of something really strong. Not necessarily in that order."

Gina gave her a wicked look. "Or a few hours in bed with the mighty fine detective. That'll perk you right up. Or make you not give a damn. Either way." She fluttered her lashes and sighed.

"I shouldn't have said anything." Her rueful smile faded. "Not that I have anything to worry about at this point. I imagine he isn't wasting any time recommending my dismissal to his commissioner, who will run right to the mayor." She shook her head.

"For God's sake, what happened? What went wrong?"

"I underestimated the power of sex."

"I never underestimate the power of sex." Gina was as well versed in how to get things done as Erin, perhaps even more so. "And neither do you. So what gives?"

"I thought I had it under control today, Gina. But it was awful. Like an ambush. I should have been prepared for the chance that the information would leak."

"Uh-oh. They found out about the pink tutu, huh?"

Erin groaned and nodded. "And the leather mask, the bustier, even the handcuffs. The only thing that didn't leak was the feather whip."

"I thought they'd kept that info locked tight."

Erin rubbed her temples. "Well, something that sensational, someone just couldn't keep his or her mouth shut. I should have been prepared. I was ready to handle the inevitable questions on the location. But the clothes...I knew it was going to come out eventually, but I'd hoped to have already pumped up Sanderson's importance to the community and how devastating his loss will be to so many charitable organizations. That way, when the inevitable cavalcade of demands for all the sordid details hit, we'd already have a solid foundation in place. I honestly didn't think it would come out this fast."

Gina swore under her breath. "Well, that sucks."

"It was madness out there, Gina. They were rabid. Worse than a pack of wolves." She rubbed her arms. "I feel unclean."

"That bad, huh?"

"Worse then when we handled that shock jock, Harold Seaman's, account."

Gina winced and whistled. "Wow, that's pretty bad."

"I tried to maintain our position, but they wouldn't even listen. You wouldn't believe the kind of stuff some of those guys asked me. Right there on the steps of city hall. And I consider myself a fairly cosmopolitan kind of girl, but honestly they shocked even me."

"Men are pigs," Gina said matter-of-factly. "They'd live with their minds in the gutter all the time if we women didn't demand at least the veneer of civility from them. But I'm telling you, Erin, that's all it is. A veneer. Underneath it's always about big boobs, nice butts, how long those legs are and won't they wrap just fine around my waist. It's sex. That's what drives them all."

"I believe just moments ago you were the one urging me to rip the veneer off and take one of those pigs out for a spin."

Gina grinned, shameless as usual. "Well, as long as you're in control of things, they *can* be useful. I mean, just because they're pigs doesn't mean we should have to make do without them. Why should our needs suffer?"

Erin just shook her head. She and Gina had had this talk many times. Both of them had been through several pretty rocky relationships and despaired of ever meeting Mr. Nice Guy. Gina had since decided to enjoy a string of Mr. Right Nows. She seemed happy enough.

After Erin's last breakup, she'd seriously wondered if her best friend didn't have the right idea. And now, while they were working so hard to build their new business, it was just as well that neither of them got serious about anyone anyway. Not that this was a problem for either of them at the moment.

Blue eyes and a cocky smile flashed through her mind.

"Well," Erin said, pushing that image right out of her mind, "it gets worse. I got a message about five minutes after I managed to escape that the mayor wants to see me in his office in two hours." She looked at her watch. "That was three Alka-Seltzers and forty-five minutes ago. I was hoping to get to Brady first, make sure he wasn't already on the warpath to get me fired."

"You should stick it to him over the leak. I'm betting it was the police. Those guys can't keep anything sealed." She laughed dryly and held up her hand. "No, don't even go there. I know I left myself wide open on that one."

Erin merely sighed. "Don't worry. I'm too upset to be a smart-ass at the moment."

Now Gina did look concerned. "You don't really think the mayor would drop you. It's not your fault those guys dug up the dirt. You ran your plan by the mayor and he approved it."

"Still, I should have seen it coming."

Gina didn't bother to argue. They were both too stubborn. "Fine. So let's stop beating ourselves up here and focus on a solution. Did you call Brady? You could set up a meeting on the way to the mayor's office. Or at least confirm he's not out there trying to tear you down."

"I tried on the cell on the way back here. He's out on the case, didn't respond to my call. Or the messages I left." She blew out a deep breath as she spun her briefcase around and opened it. "I guess I'd better figure out what I'm going to tell the mayor that will save our butts."

"You'll figure something out. You always do."

Erin rolled her eyes. "Gee, thanks for all the help."

Gina grinned as she headed for the door. "That's why they pay me the big bucks." She paused in the doorway. "Besides, I'll have my hands full trying to figure out a way to keep Tony from blaming me for what happened with his news director. Did I mention I hate insecure men?" She rolled her eyes, then ducked back to her own office.

The space they'd rented was pricey, so it was small. Just enough for their two offices, a small reception area and a tiny file room that doubled as their break room. Gina had managed to negotiate a good enough deal to get them into the trendy section of town, but the rent still sucked up all their overhead allocation. So they dealt with not being able to hire a secretary, file clerk or receptionist.

Actually, it wasn't so bad and they both equally pitched in. Ever since the first day they'd realized they both dreamed of careers in public relations, Erin and Gina had spent endless hours planning this business, right down to the carpeting and watercolors on the wall. After eighteen months, things were moving along well, but they knew they had a good two or three more years of growth before they could safely say they'd realized a solid foundation to their dream.

Both were willing to give a great deal to make that dream a reality, and give they did, often at the expense of anything resembling a real life. But they were having the time of their lives building a dream. And that was a pretty good life in and of itself, wasn't it?

"Most days anyway," Erin muttered. No one liked the down days, but this one bugged her more than most. This job for the mayor was the first time they'd been given such a high-profile opportunity to showcase their talents. And she was this close to ruining it.

She had just rewound her mini-recorder and was set to relive those lovely, excruciating moments on the city hall steps—hoping to find something, anything, to save her butt with—when a light knock on the door made her jump. She quickly stabbed at the off button, but not fast enough.

"What, you didn't get clobbered badly enough the first go-around?" Brady strolled into her office space. Space that became increasingly smaller with every step he took. It wasn't that he was such a huge man, although he did fill out the shoulders of that jacket without additional padding. He just had…presence.

"I don't remember you being a glutton for punishment," he continued, then smiled. "Unless you were the one dishing it out, of course."

"I'm not," she said curtly, too on edge to banter with him. "So if you came here to rub my nose in it, don't bother. Mayor Henley will be taking care of that little chore shortly." Erin tried not to roll her chair backward as he came right up to her desk. She hated being caught off guard like this. If by some miracle she survived losing the mayor's account, she was definitely going to find the money to hire a receptionist.

"I didn't come here to gloat," he said. "That street brawl masquerading as a press conference pissed me off every bit as much as I imagine it did you."

That steadied her. "So, the leak is from your end?"

"I have no idea. I won't pretend we haven't had a problem in that area before, and I'm already looking into it. I put a call in to the mayor and blasted an aide of his, making damn sure it didn't come from them. I couldn't get any promises from him that it didn't, so you have that little bit of leverage."

If she looked startled, it was because she was. "And you came here to tell me? I thought I was the enemy."

"Right now the enemy are the thirty-some odd reporters and half-dozen television camera crews staked out at city hall and the station house. I don't have time to play with them. I figure that's your job."

"Oh, so now that they're being a pain, you want them dumped on me."

"They're always a pain. But now that they have more details than they were ever supposed to have—"

"You yourself said you didn't know how long the seal would hold."

"I know, but, like you, I'd hoped for at least fortyeight hours to get some of the initial canvassing done, so I'd have some answers to those questions."

"What you're saying is, you needed me out there to-day as much as the mayor did." She didn't smile when she said it, this was too serious a problem for her to make light of. Needling him just seemed to come naturally to her. As did honesty. "Which means I let you both down."

He looked at her for a long moment, then shrugged. "Honestly, I'm not sure I'd have handled it any better." His lips quirked. "In fact, I'm pretty damn sure I'd have made it a lot worse. I don't have much patience for that kind of crap. You handled them about as well as anyone would."

She covered her heart with her hand. "A compliment?" She lifted her recorder. "Can I get that on record?"

"Don't let it go to your head. There's still a major problem to be dealt with here."

"So, what do you want from me?"

"I've got an investigation to complete and until I'm convinced it's not a homicide, I'd appreciate you keeping the bloodhounds off my back."

"That may not be my concern in about, oh—" she glanced at her watch "—an hour from now."

A gleam entered his eyes. The gleam a predator got when he thought about his prey. She ignored the little shiver it sent over her. And there was no pleasure in this one. She realized right then that she'd hate to be the one Brady was hunting when he was on the job.

Off the job…?

It surprised her that her mind even went there. Right now their little hormonal two-step should be the last thing on either of their minds. And yet, she realized it was never more than a beat away from surging to the surface. Something she'd do well to remember.

"I know you," he said bluntly. "You're not going to let the mayor walk all over you. No way are you walking away from a high-profile job without one hell of a fight."

"True," she said, glad he understood that. A lot of men were put off, intimidated, by a woman who knew what she wanted and set out to get it. Brady wasn't. If anything, she thought he actually respected that aspect of her. But then, that was one thing they shared, their drive. He was only annoyed by it when it got in his way.

"So why are you here? For the pep talk?" She knew better. "I don't think so. You have something for me. What is it?"

Brady sighed. "I hate it when you do that."

"What? Figure things out before you can make a point?" She felt herself relax. Well, not relax exactly, but focus. The adrenaline was pumping again, and oddly enough, that calmed her. "I can't help it if I'm faster than you."

He walked around the side of her desk and perched on the edge of it, much in the same place Gina had moments earlier. Only this felt nothing like when Gina invaded her personal space. She allowed her chair to lean back about one click, just enough so she could hold his gaze, not enough to be perceived as a retreat.

"I'm not slow," he said evenly. "I'm methodical.

And thorough." He leaned closer, spoke more deliberately. "Less mistakes are made that way."

She tried not to swallow too hard, certain he'd notice. "Are you saying I'm rash?" She felt rash. All of a sudden she felt very rash. And hot.

There was only business in his voice, but she swore there was something else going on just behind those eyes. That something that made her want to squirm in her seat...amongst other things.

He ignored her question, but nothing else. "When you replay those questions, listen to the guy from the *Examiner*. He kept pounding at you on one of Sanderson's recent business openings. The Soap and Suds. I've looked into it. It's a Laundromat that serves beer and has a jukebox."

"You're kidding."

He shook his head. "Not kidding. But I can find no obvious link from that to where and how Sanderson was found. Someone else manages it and runs it. Mort's press release back when he opened it touted the place as a way to help establish small, independent businesses downtown."

"Sounds like him," she said. "He liked to take credit for single-handedly rejuvenating the entire urban-renewal project."

"Right. He owns a number of small businesses and has also sold a number of them to the people managing them. I just can't find where anything else was going on in this particular one. But obviously the *Examiner* guy does, or he wouldn't have quizzed you on it to see what we knew."

"I don't remember anyone quizzing me about a Laundromat beer joint."

"Just listen back over the tape. You never responded to him, but it didn't keep him from asking about it, several times. He got lost in the roar."

She looked at him. "But you heard it."

His eyes twinkled. "I am a detective."

"So you want me to what? Shake him down for you?"

Her television cop-show lingo drew a smile from him, one that did nothing to help her stabilize her heart rate.

"I want you to use your public relations skills to see what you can dig out of the guy. I figure you're close enough to his line of work that maybe he'd grant you a favor."

She batted her eyelashes at him. "You mean, if I ask real nice and say pretty please? I think I can handle it." She flipped open her folder for the notes she'd taken down after the press conference was over. Somewhere in there she'd listed the names of—

Brady shoved a business card under her nose. "Guy's name is Bradford Pitts."

"Brad Pitts?" Erin laughed. "Poor guy."

Brady just looked at her. "Anyway, that's his office number." He flipped the card over. "That one is my private number. Call me when you get something."

She took the card. "Thank you," she said, and meant it. She also liked his faith in her, but she kept that to herself. "I'll call him right after I get done groveling to Henley."

"I would pay to see you grovel."

One lethal grin and her nipples went rock hard. How did he do that anyway?

He strode to the door. "You might want to call Bradford, there, first. It might give you something to pass on to the mayor, even if he won't like hearing the information. At least he'll know you're working on it."

Erin frowned now, forgetting about hard nipples. For the moment anyway. She had a feeling she'd be remembering them about as often as she remembered that grin. "You really think this guy is onto something dirty that Sanderson might have been involved in?"

"Define dirty."

That made her pause, then smile. "Well, *I* was referring to dirty business practices, but I can see *your* mind was on leather masks and feather whips."

She swore his gaze shifted down right to the front of her blazer. It was such a brief flicker, she couldn't be sure. No way he could have known about her nipples.

His eyes steady on hers, he said, "My mind is on whatever connection Sanderson might have had to his possible killer. He was found handcuffed wearing satin and leather. Just because there was no sexual intercourse doesn't mean Morty didn't naturally get his kicks from dressing up like a slutty ballerina."

Erin choked on a laugh. "Yeah. Okay." Then she couldn't help herself. "Maybe he'd have been better off opening a dry cleaner. Must have been hell keeping those tutus clean."

Brady's mouth twitched, but he conquered the urge

to smile. "We cover all the bases, Erin. Even ones that won't make the mayor happy."

"We?"

Brady sighed. "Just call me after you talk to Mr. Pitts."

Erin nodded, but she was smiling when he left her office.

Gina popped her head back in. "Detective Hunk in the oh-so-beautiful flesh? To what did we owe that honor?"

"He's being forced to play with me and he hates it." She stared at the empty doorway. "Kind of." She raised her palm. "I don't want to hear it, so just go back to work."

Gina laughed, then wagged her finger. "I'm telling you, Erin. Kaboom. Out-of-this-world, once-in-a-lifetime fireworks potential just walked out the door. You can almost taste sex in the air in here."

"Please."

She just laughed. "All you have to do is reach for it."

"Right now I have to reach for the phone and call this reporter." Gina's instant sour expression made Erin laugh. "Yeah, I know, but Brady has a hunch this guy knows something about Sanderson."

"And he's trusting you to get it out of him?" Gina lifted one eyebrow. "Hmm. He doesn't underestimate you. He's not intimidated either, as far as I can tell. He's a smart cop our Detective Hunk is." With a thoughtful look on her face that made Erin groan, Gina waved and left.

Just as Erin went to lift the phone, Gina stuck her head back around the door frame. "Kaboom, Erin." She lifted her hand. "That's all I'm sayin'. Kaboom doesn't happen too often."

5

BRADY SNATCHED the phone up on the third ring. "Homicide, O'Keefe."

"I love it when you get all authoritarian on me."

Two second ago Brady would have bet money that nothing could make him smile that day. Leave it to Erin to even the odds. Maybe even swing them in her favor. Still, he kept the smile out of his voice. "What did you find out?"

"No, no, the mayor didn't fire me after all, but thank you for asking."

Brady sighed, wondering how she could annoy and arouse him at the same time. And so often! "I didn't ask because I knew Henley wouldn't let you go."

"Well, in this case your faith exceeded mine." Her tone turned dry. "Rare, I know, but thanks."

"You're welcome." He liked that about her, too. She pulled no punches when dishing it out, but neither did she put on any pretenses when the focus was on her. "So, what did you get?"

"You're like a bulldog," she said, but went on without waiting for a response. "I did talk to Pitts. And by the way, he's as lovely a human being as his last name would indicate."

Brady swore he would not laugh. Smiling was one

thing, but dammit, he was in the middle of a homicide investigation, here. And all his instincts were beginning to scream at him that this was indeed a homicide. "Yeah, a real peach of a guy, I'm sure. What did you get out of him?"

"Again with the faith. I'm going to have to start hanging out with you more often. Listen," she went on. "I have to make a few more calls and check in with the mayor. Is there any way we could meet and discuss this later?"

"Calls? About this? Erin, I'm the detective here. Don't get carried away with this."

"I can take care of myself, Detective."

He swore under his breath. "You didn't answer my question. Are the calls regarding the conversation with Pitts? If so, I want all the details. Now. I'll make the calls."

"Just give me a time when we can meet."

He sighed and swore again.

"Very...inventive, Detective."

He did not smile. He did not. "You make me crazy."

"Well, that makes two of us."

Brady paused then. He'd meant crazy in the purest sense of the word. At least this time he had. But there had been another layer to her response. Hadn't there? Or was that just wishful thinking?

Oh yeah, like he needed to get more tangled up with her. What was he, nuts?

He let his forehead sink onto his hand. "Seven o'clock. Jimmy's, over on Tenth. You know it?"

"No, but I can find it. I'll be there."

Brady hung up the phone, knowing he should only be looking forward to this meeting for the information she was about to give him. Which was why he totally refused to give in to the urge to comb his hair and straighten his tie. Hell, where was his tie anyway?

JIMMY'S WAS a small pizza and beer joint with a decent-size jumbo screen and a satellite dish that pulled in sports channels from all over. It wasn't a cop hangout, which made it even more perfect for Brady. He saw enough cops at work. Brady had found this place a year or so ago when he'd interviewed a subject. He came here when he needed the noise, a cold beer and no phones ringing, so he could think out the particulars of a case that was bugging him. He'd never shared Jimmy's with anyone. It was sort of like his hideout. Silly, really. No reason inviting Erin here should feel personal. It wasn't as if he owned the joint.

Then she came strolling in. And Lord, did the lady have a stroll on her. He smiled as he noticed the heads at the small counter swivel in her direction. About the only time he could recall that ever happening here. And during Monday-night football, too. Not that he could blame them.

She sent a smile their way and asked the score. The four men all but fell over themselves to give her the details.

"I don't think the Eagles defense has a prayer against anyone in the central division," she responded thoughtfully. "But they ought to handle our own well enough, Giants included. So unless they get their passing game in gear, New York won't beat them tonight. Now, Pittsburgh next Sunday? Trouble there, guys, take my word on it." She grinned, they gaped, then she said goodbye and headed toward his table.

Brady shook his head as she sat down across from him. "You realize you could probably get four marriage proposals right this minute without even putting out for it."

She covered her heart with her hand. "You mean you're a Steelers' fan, too? I might pop the question myself."

"Steelers?" He looked properly horrified.

Erin laughed. "Well, I see that's one less heart I won't be breaking."

Brady smiled. "Just as well. We won't have to divorce when the Eagles march to the Super Bowl, leaving the Steelers in their dust."

Her eyes narrowed. "You don't really want to go there."

His smile spread to a grin. "No, not really. I hate to see a grown woman cry."

"Oh, a funny guy. You're really gunning for it now."

He leaned back. "Yeah, well, we'll see who's gunning for who come January."

She merely held his gaze with a steely-eyed one of her own. "Did you invite me here to insult my intelligence with your incredibly narrow-minded, not to mention delusional, opinions on the world's greatest sport? Or are we supposed to be conducting some business?"

Oh, she was fun to rile. Way too much fun. But her

comment did bring him back to the reason they were here. It probably wasn't a good sign that he kind of resented the intrusion of business. He couldn't remember the last time fun and relaxation had taken any kind of precedence over work. Probably because it never had.

He straightened and pulled the pitcher toward him. "You like beer?"

"Sure."

Brady got up and snagged a frosted mug from Miller, the old guy that ran the counter, then settled once again across from her. "Pizza should be out in a few minutes. I didn't know what you liked, so I got it loaded and figured you could just pick off what you don't want."

Her lips twitched. "I bet you make a charming date in a fine restaurant."

"I get around that by never dining in fine restaurants."

"Good strategy."

They really had to stop this. Problem was, the longer they baited each other, the harder it was for him to remember why.

She took a sip of her beer and he found it almost impossible not to watch her throat work. Slender throat for such a strong-willed woman, he found himself thinking.

"Like I told you, I talked to Pitts," she said.

Well, that takes care of that daydream. Brady pulled his gaze back to his own beer and told himself to get back

on the stick. "What did you find out? What calls did
you have to make? Did you find a link?"

"You sure you wouldn't rather be in an interroga-
tion room? The glare of a single bulb? Tiny bamboo
slivers?"

"You forgot the rubber hose. I especially like the
rubber hose."

She put her palms up. "Okay, okay. You're too good
at this. I have to work too hard to keep up with you."

Business, Detective. Get down to business. And still he
was damned if his eyes didn't stray past the pitcher,
past her beer mug, to the way her fingers toyed with
the gold chain that dipped between her breasts. *Jesus,
he needed to get out more.*

"I try," he said finally. "So do I have to feed you first
to get you to talk, or what?"

As if he'd conjured the pizza, it arrived right then.
Steaming and hot and smelling out of this world. Well,
at least it gave him a legit reason to drool.

"Looks great," she said, breathing deeply. "I like the
old-fashioned thin crust. And I didn't know they came
in a rectangle anymore." Her eyes lit up. "Remember
the Pizza Oven over on Third? Did your family ever
eat there?"

Brady nodded. "We did. I loved Alby's pizza. A real
shame his sons sold the place after he died."

"Agreed. Well, if this is half as good as his, Jimmy's
has a new customer for life."

Brady could have told her it was maybe even better
than Alby's. He wasn't sure how he felt about her coming in and out of here when he might be here. He

shouldn't have brought her. Once this case was over, it'd be better if they just went back to their own anonymous lives. She was far too big a distraction. So big, in fact, he was having a hell of a time shoving it aside and focusing on the job. That alone set off warning bells louder than a police siren.

Then she was moaning as she chewed her first bite. He knew she had no idea just how ridiculously turned on he got over that little heartfelt moan. Which only made him all the more pathetic. He was definitely going to find time to go out more. With anyone. Anywhere.

Erin motioned to the guy behind the counter. "Is he the owner?"

Brady looked at Miller, then back at Erin. "No, he just runs the counter."

"But he makes the pizza?"

Brady nodded. "Yeah, why?"

"I think I'm going to marry him. This pizza and big-screen football." She sighed. "What more could a girl ask for?"

Brady refused to even go there, not even the tiniest little bit. He had half a notion to get up and walk out now, cut his losses, run like hell.

But he didn't. And he wasn't keen on the realization that him staying put wasn't entirely because of his dedication to the job.

"If you're all done planning the honeymoon, can we please talk about Pitts and the connection he found between the laundry joint and Sanderson's death?"

Erin made a face. "Spoilsport. I can't remember the

last time I just hung out in a pizza joint and watched the game. But if you insist we act like responsible adults with jobs to do, who am I to ruin your fun?"

His lips twitched. He focused on his pizza. He was astonished to see a third of the pie was gone. "Damn, you really do like pizza."

"Girl's got to keep something in her tank for fuel."

If he'd hoped to irk her, and maybe he had, to get back on combat ground where he felt more comfortable, she didn't let him get away with it. Any other woman on the face of the planet would have had his balls in a sling for a comment that even indirectly referred to the possibility she was enjoying her food too much. Not Erin.

"Well, thanks for saving some fuel for my tank." It had come out more gruffly than he'd planned, but dammit, he was on the ropes here.

She pushed the pan closer to him. "I'm done. You eat while I talk."

Probably the wisest course of action left, he thought. So he nodded and pulled a piece off the pan.

She poured more beer for both of them, then settled back in her chair. "Pitts is an ass. But he's also a guy."

Brady raised his eyebrows, but wisely said nothing.

"Guys like Pitts can never seem to get past the notion that women have breasts first and brains second."

Brady choked on his pizza. And yanked his gaze firmly away from the little black sweater she was wearing.

She pushed his mug at him. "Are you okay? Here, have a sip." She leaned back again once she was certain he wasn't dying. "Anyway, getting information out of this guy wasn't exactly brain surgery." She grinned. "More like boob surgery."

"I think this is more information than I need to know."

She shrugged. "Just telling you what happened."

"Just get to the meat of it."

"I won't even touch that one."

Brady had to laugh at the unintentional opening he'd given her. "I owe you one then."

"And don't you think I won't collect." Before he could respond, she settled back again with her mug. "Apparently the Soap and Suds changed hands several times before Sanderson came into possession of it. Did you look back into that?"

"Only as far back as his purchase. He bought it from an Asian couple who was moving out of state to be closer to their only child when she went to college. Out West somewhere."

"Did you know it belonged to the wife's family before that? It was sort of a wedding present to her new husband. It was called Hans' Laundry."

Brady nodded. "I think I made a note of that, yeah. Sanderson changed it to the Soap and Suds idea and hired a couple of young people to run it. What's the connection to Sanderson's death?"

Erin sat her mug on the table and leaned forward, dropping her voice. "Well, Pitts wasn't exactly a fountain of information. But he made a reference to the Han family's other business."

Brady was all ears now, his mind firmly back on work. "What other business?"

"Apparently they also own several video stores."

Brady just looked at her. "And this is important why?"

Erin smiled. "Do you have any idea how hard it is to rent really good Asian porn in this city?"

"Christ. Sanderson was involved in some sort of underground video-porn deal with the Hans?"

Erin shrugged. "I have no idea. I'm not the detective. I don't know if Sanderson even knew about their other businesses. He bought the Laundromat from their son-in-law and might have no idea what the wife's family was dealing in. It was just the sex angle that caught my eye, seeing how Sanderson was found and all. This could be a total dead end. I don't think Pitts has it all figured out either. He was looking into Sanderson's various business dealings trying to find something. Maybe he's written something on the Hans in the past, so the link rang a bell. They've been tied to underground porn distribution, but I did a quick scan of headlines in the local papers for the last couple of years at the library and it yielded nothing more than suspicions. I didn't see any sensational courtroom dramas."

"I thought you were letting me do the detecting?"

"Honestly, Brady, I spent an hour in the public library. That's hardly sleuthing. Probably there is nothing to this and Pitts was just fishing."

Brady looked at her. "Does Pitts know about the porn?"

She propped her chin on her hands, her gaze

steadily on his. "Not directly. He only commented on the video-store ownership. But what other reason would tweak his suspicions?"

"So you came up with this angle by yourself?"

"Gina helped me." At his look, she just gave it right back to him. "Hey, all we did was look up the video stores in the Yellow Pages. Sanderson was found in a sexually explicit manner, so if the Hans' stores are somehow related, then it figures that the only sex-related thing in a video store is usually porn."

"But you said Asian porn."

"Well, that was Gina's angle. She figured they'd have to have some special market." Her eyes sparked. "So we dropped by one of the locations. I talked to the counter help while Gina sneaked into the members-only room they had in the back. I have no idea on the legality of it or anything, but Asian porn is definitely their specialty."

Brady sat back. "I want your nose, and Gina's, completely out of this as of right now. Understand?"

He should have never asked her the simple favor. He should have known nothing was ever simple with Erin. If this was more than the Hans simply importing a few overseas videos, it could mean something far more dangerous. There were some Asian families the equal of mob families when it came to certain types of organized crime. Only, they were much harder to crack. And far more vicious with their enemies.

Erin lifted her hands in surrender. "Hey, I don't live for this kind of thing." She smiled. "Gina kind of liked it, though." At Brady's glare she quickly added, "But it's all yours, tough guy. We're out of it."

"So we have an understanding?"

"I've got enough to deal with regarding the mayor."

"Speaking of that, just what did you tell Henley about all this?"

"Nothing. He agreed that the leak might have come from city hall. He is deeply concerned about his campaign, but, for the moment anyway, doesn't blame me for the fiasco of a press conference. His campaign manager, however, thinks otherwise. He'd like to see me walk, but only because he resented my intrusion in the first place."

"You didn't tell him about the video thing?"

She shook her head. "Since we don't know where the leak is, I figured you didn't need any more info getting out than necessary. And I don't see where the information is going to be useful to the mayor anyway. What is most useful is you getting to the bottom of the case and making it go away. I will say that, moron or not, Pitts is likely to put this together like we did and run some kind of piece anyway. So my being quiet with the mayor may be moot."

"Yeah." Brady sighed heavily and pushed his chair back. "Thank you for the help."

She stood as well. "All in a day's work."

Brady tossed some bills on the table. "What are your plans as far as the mayor is concerned?"

Erin waved to the guys at the counter, then trailed Brady to the door. "Well, first off, no more press conferences. Not until you have something more solid."

"The press will run rampant with what they do have."

She snorted and passed through the door he held for her. "Like I don't know that. But talking to them isn't making it better. I will work with Fletcher, Henley's campaign guy, on focusing the mayor on campaign issues and off of Sanderson completely. Our official word is 'We have no comment other than to say this is a police matter, and we're confident they are handling things.'"

"Gee, thanks," Brady said.

"Hey, you said you could handle them."

"Yeah." For the first time he actually wished she would take the media on for him. His head was spinning in ten different directions. With the information she'd just given him, he'd be up all night tracking down stuff. His gut told him it was the right direction. God only knew what he'd find at the bottom of his investigation. But he already had a feeling about it. A bad feeling. The last thing he felt like dealing with was the press.

Erin stepped to the corner, looking for a taxi.

"I can give you a lift," he said. "My cruiser is in the back lot."

She turned, her smile faltering for the first time that night. Interesting. *No, no, O'Keefe. Work, no play.*

"I, um—no, that's okay. Really."

Brady grinned now. *So, she was fine in public, but not totally comfortable being in a car with him?* Apparently it was a biological thing that made it impossible for him to not exploit a weakness in her. She had so few of them.

"What, you don't want to play with my siren and listen to copspeak on the radio?"

Her poise returned instantly. He was only partly disappointed. As much as her occasional weak moment intrigued him, he preferred it when they were evenly matched.

"You really know how to show a girl a good time, O'Keefe. Just a helpful hint, you might want to leave it at the pizza and football."

"Some women like the police toys."

She visibly swallowed and Brady had to bite down on a wider grin.

"Not this woman. You can keep your leather belts and silver bracelets to yourself."

"Well, I think my feelings are hurt."

"I didn't think you had feelings."

"Now I know they are." They both laughed. "Come on, the cruiser is over here."

She finally nodded and they walked to the back lot. Brady got her settled in the unmarked sedan then got in the other side.

"Wow," she said, looking over the high-tech dashboard. "You do have cool toys."

He smiled. "Works every time."

She only rolled her eyes.

"Where to?"

"Actually, you can take me back to the office."

Brady nodded and turned out of the lot. Another thing they had in common. They were both workaholics. It was just as well he didn't know where she lived anyway. Keep things as separate as possible. He kept telling himself that all the way across town.

"So, how is it you don't have the requisite two-point-three kids, golden retriever and white picket fence?" she asked after the silence had stretched for several blocks.

He didn't ask how she knew he was single. It was hardly a secret. "Police officers and marriage make a bad mix," he said, keeping his eyes off the long legs she kept shifting and squarely on the road.

"You speak from authority then?"

"Not the way you mean. I watched what it did to my family and too many of my friends on the force. It was one lesson I avoided learning the hard way."

"Pretty cynical outlook."

"Pretty cynical job."

She didn't say anything to that.

"So how about you," he asked after he'd just gotten done telling himself he wouldn't.

She shrugged. "I've been pretty focused on getting my business up and running. It doesn't leave much room for relationship building." Dry amusement filled her voice as she added, "Plus, most of the men I meet are jerks."

Brady glanced over at her. "So it's just a matter of meeting Mr. Right, then? Or does business come first?"

"Oh, I definitely plan to settle down one day."

"As long as he isn't a jerk."

She laughed. "Exactly. But I don't plan to make my job my life. There's more to life than work. I mean, at some point the job ends. And if that's all you built, then what do you have?"

"Memories of a damn fine career and the difference you made in the lives of other people," he responded easily.

Her amused look faded. "Doesn't do much to keep your toes warm on a long winter's night."

"That's what big hound dogs are for."

"You have a dog?"

He glanced at her, a tiny bit miffed that she sounded so surprised. Which was absurd since he didn't have a dog. "I barely manage to feed and walk myself regularly. I was talking about later on. After retirement." He'd make a great dog owner then. Just not now.

She folded her arms. "You can't even fathom that day, can you? When you have nothing to get up for except walking the dog."

He started to shoot off his mouth again, but something stopped him. Maybe it was the surprise at how easily she seemed to read him. "No, no, I can't," he said, as honest as he'd ever been. He pulled over to the curb in front of her building. "Nice digs," he said, changing the subject. Running like hell from this one.

Thankfully she let him. "Gina got us a good deal. You know what they say. 'Location, location, location.'"

"How long have you been here?"

"Almost two years. We're doing okay."

"But this job for the mayor would make things a lot more okay, wouldn't it?"

She looked at him squarely. "Absolutely." She

opened her door. "So give us both a career boost and go catch a killer for me."

He smiled briefly and nodded. "That's my job." They both knew he could just as well have said, "That's my life."

She leaned in then, her expression surprisingly earnest. "There should be more than that, Brady. You can't be just a cop. Even as good a one as you are. It's not enough." She stood then and snapped the door shut, effectively ending the conversation and neatly giving her the last word.

Not that he cared. He pulled back into traffic, his mind firmly on the tasks that lay before him in the hours ahead. He hardly thought about what she'd said at all.

What the hell did she know about it anyway? She was still single, focused intently on her career. They weren't so different. Except she still had hope for happily-ever-after.

Well, she hadn't seen the ravages police work wreaked on marriages firsthand the way he had. And second and third hand. His own parents, his uncle and many of his squad had suffered, and it had been plenty ugly for all involved. He was just being smart by staying single. His life was plenty full without all that hoopla.

He pulled into the lot behind the station house and walked to his desk and the pile of work that waited for him. Yeah, his life was plenty full.

6

"DID YOU SEE the headlines in today's papers? Gina came sailing into Erin's office and plopped a thick stack of newspapers on her desk. "'Sanderson Sells Sex on the Side.'" She snorted. "More like, 'Sex Sells Newspapers.' Hypocrites."

Erin groaned. It had been three days since her pizza-and-beer meeting with Brady. Three days of headlines screaming about Sanderson being tied in to a porn ring. Pitts had wasted no time. She hadn't heard from Brady, but she'd seen him on the news, ducking reporters on his way in and out of the station house and city hall. He was the hot target now that it was clear the mayor was making no further comments on the case, through her or anyone else.

Which didn't mean her job for Henley had lightened up at all. She and Fletcher had been in lengthy meetings, and when they weren't meeting physically, they were on conference calls. She'd been busy working on press releases and radio spots that would be focusing on the mayor's campaign issues. And carefully skirting the support he'd gotten from Morton Sanderson.

She was quickly discovering that getting people to talk about substantive election issues was much harder than getting people to not talk about sex and Morton Sanderson.

"I'm beginning to wish I'd never taken on this job."

"Bite your tongue. Our firm's name has been plastered in the papers for almost a week straight now."

Erin eyed her balefully. "I'm not certain that's a plus."

"What kind of public relations person are you?" Gina folded her arms. "The first thing they taught us was that any PR can be turned into good PR."

"Well, I'm tired of finding ways to make this bad press look good. It all stinks, Gina. Even if it turns out Sanderson was murdered, it doesn't look like it's going to be because he was some kind of Boy Scout."

"You don't know that. And you've done a good job of distancing the mayor from the matter." When Erin merely stared at her, she relented. "Okay, so the distance isn't that great yet, but you're working on it."

Erin didn't want to talk about this anymore. She finally had two hours to work on anything else but the mayor, and she wasn't going to spend it talking about him. "Everything turn out all right with Tony?" she asked.

Gina nodded, but blew out a long breath. "I swear, if the man gets that job in New York, it will be in spite of himself. He'd better send some business our way, because getting him that job will mostly be my doing." She brightened. "Speaking of that, we are getting some calls for work. Mostly political stuff."

Erin groaned. "I think I'd rather work with the Tonys of the world than another politician."

"You'll think differently when the money and referrals are coming in."

Erin had to nod. "You're probably right. After all, how many politicians can there be connected to Asian-mob porn rings and with predilections for pink tutus and bustiers?"

"Probably more than you'd like to know."

They both laughed as Gina walked back to the door. "I've got a meeting with a councilman from one of the outlying districts this afternoon. He says his constituents think he's too stiff and starchy."

"Well, if anyone can take the starch out of him, it's you, my friend."

Gina gave a sassy wink. "You got that right, sister."

Erin chuckled as the door clicked shut. Her smile faded as her gaze fell back on the pile of newspapers Gina had deposited on her desk. One by one she scooped them up and aimed them at her trash can. A photo below the fold on one of the papers caught her eye however.

It was Brady, ducking into his cruiser. She smiled at the image. His expression made it clear he was not thrilled with being hounded. His jaw was set, his lips tight, eyes straight ahead. That was Brady. Eyes always straight ahead.

She thought about their conversation just before she got out of his car the other night. His views on relationships and marriage were pretty hard-nosed, but she understood why he held them. She couldn't imagine being married to a guy whose work meant as much, if not more to him, than anything else. Including his wife and family.

Still, she'd enjoyed working with him, helping him out, even as briefly as she had. Not that she had any burning desire to go into detective work, but she'd liked being involved, talking about it, theorizing. These past couple of days had been a nightmare of work for her, and yet she'd found herself thinking more than once about the pizza and beer they'd shared. She found herself wishing she could call him up and ask him to meet her at Jimmy's so they could talk over both of their situations. She could get his feedback on some of her ideas on how to help the mayor, and listen to what he'd come up with regarding the murder.

She shook her head with a self-deprecating laugh. Who was she kidding? She wasn't thinking business, she was thinking romance. "Baaaad idea, Erin." Hell, Brady couldn't have been clearer on the issue of romance and his total disinterest in it. Actually, he'd been talking about marriage, not romance. But still, it was all the same.

Wasn't it? One side of her brain parried with the other. What if she wasn't really talking about romance? What if she was strictly talking the physical side of a relationship? After all, that was what her hormones were really in a stir about anyway. Even if he was antimarriage, the man probably wasn't a monk, at least she couldn't imagine he was. He had to have some sort of release outside of work. She shivered a little at the word *release*. So, okay, she'd spent a teensy bit of time fantasizing about Detective Hunk. What red-blooded woman wouldn't? Besides, she deserved some form of entertainment after the days she'd put in, right?

She should be working on a press release for an author who was doing a local morning talk show. And yet her mind wouldn't budge off of Brady.

She wasn't a monk, either. Or a nun, or whatever. Didn't she deserve a release valve, too? Fantasizing was enjoyable enough, but it was no replacement for the real thing. And it had been a while since the real thing had been part of her life. *Whoa, Erin. Stop right there.* But she didn't want to stop there. She wanted…well, she wanted Brady. Not for life or anything. She grinned privately. Just for the night would be fine.

There, she'd admitted it. And instead of sending her running in the opposite direction, she found the idea…compelling. Attractive even. Yes, there were definite risks, though she didn't think her heart, much less his, would be one of them. She respected him, and thought he felt the same. She was definitely attracted to him and felt pretty certain he was to her. He alternately intrigued and irritated her just often enough to keep it interesting without the threat of it getting too serious.

Best of all; he had zero desire to have anything resembling a real relationship with anyone. And she wasn't really in the market for commitment either. In other words, they were the perfect couple. They could be each other's release valve.

She looked at the computer screen and the font selection she was currently trying to decide on, but all she saw was the two of them, together...releasing each other. When she tried to type, her fingers slid on the keyboard. Her palms were actually damp. She finally gave up and closed her eyes. *Could she go through with a plan like this? Did she dare?*

She opened her eyes and laughed at herself. Just what the hell did she think she was going to do? Logically outline the plan to Brady and expect him to calmly agree? Or simply invite him over for an evening of wine and a rousing bout of tension-releasing sex? *Yeah, right.*

Or maybe she'd simply seduce him into saying yes?

That stopped her cold. Sure, she'd used her femininity to get things done, but she was no femme fatale.

A knock at her door had her jumping in her seat. She knew that knock.

"Come in." She cleared her throat when that came out in a strangled whisper. "Come in, please."

Brady popped the door open and stepped in. He looked much the same as he had in the newspaper picture. Five o'clock shadow, finger-combed hair, tense jaw. And that suit. She wondered if he simply slept in it so he'd always be ready when justice called, or if he bought his suits at Rumpled-R-Us. Oddly, the look worked for him. Added to his rugged, roguish allure.

"Something amusing?"

She shook her head, wishing he couldn't read her so easily. But any lingering plans for seduction were firmly pushed aside as well. What had she been thinking anyway? This was a man who thought only of police work with every breath he took. If she so much as mentioned her release-valve idea to him he'd probably be shocked, then laugh himself sick. Thank God she'd come back to her senses.

"What brings you here?" she asked, proud of her brisk, businesslike tone. She would not, under any circumstances, allow herself to picture the two of them naked, entwined and...releasing. Absolutely not.

"You have a few minutes?" His voice was as endearingly rough and rumpled as the rest of him.

She had to purposefully ignore the urge to clench her thighs together against the ache that seemed to plague her every time he was around. "Find out something new to torture me and the mayor with?"

Brady didn't smile at her jibe. In fact, he looked more serious than she ever recalled seeing him. Which was really saying something for super cop here.

Erin forgot all about clenching thighs and release valves. Frowning, she propped her elbows on her desk. "What happened?"

He crossed the room and sank heavily into the chair. *Uh-oh. This didn't look good.* When he didn't say anything right off, she gave him a minute or two, but finally said, "Just spit it out, for God's sake."

Brady looked at her, then looked away, then finally heaved a sigh and looked back at her again. "Sanderson's death was a homicide. I just got the labs back."

"So the heart attack wasn't natural causes?"

He shook his head.

"You suspected this all along though, right? So, what's wrong?"

"It took a while for them to trace it. A little-known

pharmaceutical was introduced into his system. It acts like digitalis."

She had no idea what he was getting at. "And?"

"This particular pharmaceutical is actually more like a medicinal herb. Rare and not much is known about its properties in the United States. It's typically imported."

Her shoulders drooped. "Let me guess. Asia."

"Got it in one."

"So have you brought the Hans in for questioning?"

"Right now we can't make any connection between them and Sanderson. Other than their daughter and son-in-law owned a business he eventually bought. The daughter and son-in-law have apparently severed all ties with their family. At least businesswise. And we have no links at all direct from Sanderson to the Han empire or even to the Hans privately, separate from any business relationship. Other than buying their son-in-law's business, Sanderson apparently never dealt in any way with the Han family."

"So now what?"

Looking thoroughly frustrated, he shrugged. "We keep digging. My gut tells me this is the right path. That Morton was tied into them in some way, a way that led to him ending up dead. There was no sexual activity, so the scene was intended to humiliate him after his death."

"Like killing him wasn't bad enough?"

Brady shook his head. "You see, that's part of the culture, too. At least in some segments of it anyway, personal humiliation can be considered an even greater shame than a dishonorable death."

"And you're betting the Hans share that belief?"

"Yes, I am. But that's not enough to hang anything more than an instinct and suspicion on. I have to have more than that to bring them in."

"So you have questioned them."

"At length. It was part of the investigation. They weren't brought in as suspects. People aren't as forthcoming if they think they're suspects."

"They must have thought it curious they were being questioned."

"They thought we were merely checking into all of Sanderson's businesses. Of course, they knew we'd be somewhat suspicious of any link to them due to their rumored connection to the Asian mob scene."

"So did they seem nervous or anything?"

He shook his head. "No, but that's not surprising. They know we don't have anything concrete."

"Do they know you traced the herb or whatever was used to kill Sanderson?"

Again he shook his head. "We are trying to find something that would tie them directly to access to that herb. But while it's relatively uncommon, it's sold in some Asian marketplaces, including several in this city. We have people working on that right now." His fingers curled into fists. "But I know this is the path. I've just got to find the link, the proof."

Erin leaned back in her chair, somewhat awed by the task he took on every day. That of standing up for justice, digging up the dirt, finding the bad guy. Being responsible for making sure someone paid for the wrongs done.

"What did the mayor say about this development?" she asked.

"Nothing. He doesn't know the details, only that we've confirmed Sanderson's death as a homicide. The commissioner is playing this one close. We won't risk a leak this time."

"So why tell me?"

He looked at her, then down at his hands. "Yeah, well."

She waited, but he didn't say anything else. Then she realized why he'd been so reluctant moments ago. She stood and came around in front of her desk. Leaning back against it, she folded her arms. "You need my help again, right? Well, I hate to let you down when it obviously cost you to come here, but I don't have any connections in that sector at all." She smiled. "I mean, some of my clients have had problems with pharmaceuticals, but I don't think that will help you out much in this case."

After a moment, Brady stood and headed for the door. "This was a bad idea."

Totally confused now, Erin called out, "Wait a minute. What was that all about?"

He stopped, but it was a moment before he turned back to her. When he did, he simply held her gaze, and continued to do so for the longest time. The tension in the room climbed steadily as the seconds ticked away.

"Brady?" she asked uncertainly. It might be her earlier thoughts playing mind tricks on her, but the tension between them right now felt decid-edly...nonbusinesslike.

"I must be crazy," he finally murmured.

She took a step closer, needing to see his eyes. What she saw in them stopped her in her tracks. *Wow*. So. Okay. As it turned out, it wasn't her mind playing tricks on her after all.

She took a shaky breath. "What makes you think you're crazy?"

He stood absolutely still. But his gaze was an active, live thing, reaching out, touching her. Rocking her. How had she ever thought there would be anything re-motely safe about playing with Brady?

"I'm here, aren't I?" he said roughly.

"And?"

"I'm not supposed to be here. I'm supposed to be out there." He didn't look away, he didn't so much as blink. "But I came here."

"Yeah, yeah, you did," she said softly. Erin began to tremble. "Why?"

"I wish I knew."

So he hadn't come by to ask her for help. He'd just...come by. She forced her feet to move, to take that step. "I think maybe you have an idea." And she saw, very clearly, that he absolutely had an idea. She didn't know whether to reach for it...or run like hell.

"Yeah. Maybe I do." He watched her take another step closer. "It's a bad idea, Erin."

"Possibly."

"I should go. Now."

She walked closer. "Probably."

"I should be working."

"Absolutely." She stopped just in front of him. The tension was all but leaping from him, clawing at her. "But you're not."

He shook his head. "No. No, I'm not."

She closed that last inch between them. "Then just what are you doing, Brady?"

"Losing the rest of my mind." He all but growled the words. Then he kicked the door shut behind him and reached for her.

7

BRADY KNEW he'd regret this. But right now he didn't
give a damn. His hands were on Erin Mahoney.
Heaven help him.

She moved fluidly into his arms. Her lips were a
fiery blast that branded him clear to his toes. And her
taste...dear God, but he'd never known sin had a fla-
vor.

He leaned back against the door as the room tilted
beneath his feet. She molded her body to his as he continued to take her mouth. Her sweet, hot mouth. His
hands moved of their own volition over curves they'd
traced many times in his dreams. Dreams that were a
pale imitation of this scoring, sensual reality.

He should stop this. It wasn't too late to stop, to find
his way back to sanity, back to control. His hands
skated up her sides, his fingers brushing the sides of
her breasts. Any second now he'd let her go, step back.

Then she moaned. It came from deep in her throat
and vibrated through him. He wove his fingers
through her hair and forgot all about stopping. His
kisses were deep, dark and intensely demanding. She
didn't pull away, no, not Erin. She responded to his demands fully, then made a few of her own. And then he
was the one moaning.

Her phone buzzed. They both broke free of the kiss simultaneously and quite breathlessly.

"You—" He rasped. "You need to get that?"

"Probably." She was still plastered against him, the two of them up against the door.

His body was a rage of demands, his mind a riot of confusion. "What the hell was that we just did, Erin?"

"I have no idea." Then a dry smile curved her lips as she looked up at him. "But I wonder. Do you think we'll get even better with practice?"

He didn't know whether to laugh or groan. "Probably we shouldn't do this again." She looked at him as if he was nuts and he found himself chuckling. "Yeah, okay. But we shouldn't."

"You go first then. I'll follow your lead." She moved very slightly against him and his body leaped. "Just walk away."

"I will," he said, his voice strained. "In just a second."

She laughed now. "How is it we took so long to figure this out?"

His eyes widened. "I thought it happened pretty fast."

"Men. Always the last to know."

His eyes narrowed. "You mean, you've thought about...you know. This?"

"It will only swell your already oversize ego, but yes." She looked directly into his eyes. "Incessantly."

He swallowed against the sudden tightness in his throat. "Maybe...maybe it's crossed my mind. Once. Or a dozen times. Maybe more."

She grinned boldly now. "If it makes you feel any better, I was thinking about trying to, you know, talk to you. About this. I was afraid you'd laugh."

"You? Afraid? I don't think so." He shifted her away from him, afraid his body would betray him and explode if he didn't get her off of him.

She moved unsteadily back, finally resting against her desk. She pushed her hair off her face. "I had this plan."

He folded his arms, wishing like hell things would subside a little. His pants were quite uncomfortable at the moment. But just looking at her kept him rigid. "A plan?"

"I was thinking we are both pretty busy."

He nodded.

She tipped her head back and gazed at the ceiling. "I can't believe I'm telling you this."

"Go ahead, you've started now." *I've tasted you now.*

She glanced back to him. "It's just, neither of us have time for relationships. You don't want one and I would do just as well without one right now. But it's not like we still don't have...well, needs."

He smiled now. She was flustered. Erin Mahoney. Flustered. Who'd have thought it. "Needs, huh?"

She rolled her eyes. "Okay, don't make this harder than it is."

His smile widened to a grin. "Trust me, it couldn't be any harder."

She laughed, but her cheeks bloomed the most becoming shade of pink. Well, well. Who'd have thought he could fluster Erin *and* make her blush? He was intrigued and aroused. A very potent combination.

She recovered from her uncustomary lapse with admirable ease. "I was fairly certain you were attracted to me as I was to you." Her wry smile returned. "Alternating frequently with frustration and irritation."

"I can certainly identify with that."

"Which is why I wasn't going to do anything about it."

"What was your plan? Before you so nobly decided to abandon it." He knew his taunting was only going to go unchallenged for so long. And time was officially up.

She crossed the room, coming to stand before him again.

"You work hard. I work hard. You have a great deal of tension on a daily basis. And although mine can't compare to yours, I have my own frustrations." She reached up and toyed with his collar, then finally looked in his eyes. "I thought we both could use a release valve. Of sorts. One with no strings, no demands. Just...a safe outlet."

Brady looked into those bewitching eyes of hers, heard her oh-so-logical plan and knew he'd lost it but good when it actually sounded viable to him. Because there was nothing remotely safe about Erin Mahoney. Not intellectually and sure as hell not sexually. He knew that without doubt. And yet, even as he stood there trying to convince himself he should turn her down...he knew he wouldn't.

"Interesting plan."

She held his gaze boldly. "I thought so."

Brady looked into her eyes, really looked. But that's all he saw there. No starry-eyed dreams of romance, no ulterior motives of pulling the bait and switch when she had him well and truly hooked. All he saw was plain, honest need. And a plan to satisfy that need. With him.

He reached up and covered her hand with his, stopping her from tracing little patterns along his collar. Her touch made it hard to think. Not that thinking was going to change anything. And not because he was hard up for a release valve as she called it. The truth was, he hadn't sought one out lately for the very reasons she'd listed earlier. Women might say there wouldn't be strings, or expectations. But inevitably there were.

Erin wasn't most women. In fact, she was the only woman he'd ever met who was most decidedly her own woman.

"We'll need to set up some ground rules," he said.

The instant she realized he'd tacitly agreed to her plan, her pupils shot wide with a desire so brilliant he almost—almost—told her right then and there that she could simply name her terms and he'd agree to them.

"Rules are good," she murmured.

"Yeah." Damn if they all didn't fly right out of his mind, though. He was looking at her mouth and all he could think about was tasting her again. "This can't interfere." He said the words almost to himself.

"We'll be smart," she agreed, sounding distracted

herself. "Make it be what we want it to be. Nothing more. We're smart people after all."

"Smart," he said roughly. "Yeah." Then he gave up all pretense of keeping track of what they were talking about and pulled her to him again.

Brady was all-consuming, overwhelming her senses so fully she could drown herself...in him. And she wanted to sink under, again and again.

When he moved his mouth off her lips and began the most delicious assault along the line of her jaw, she actually began trying to figure out where they could finish what they'd started. Damn, she wished she'd opted for an office couch. Even a bigger desk would be nice at the moment.

The knock and Gina's voice came at the same time. "Erin, I need a—" She nudged the door open, then grunted when her attempt met with resistance. "Erin?"

Erin froze and so did Brady. But he didn't take his mouth, or his hands off her. She wasn't sure if that was reassuring...or mortifying. Deciding it was a little of both, she pushed at his hands first, then his chest, and eventually disentangled herself from him. She was smoothing her hair off her face as she answered. "Just a moment."

"What's going on? You sound weird."

Erin looked at Brady and was thankful he quickly looked away, or else they would have both doubled over in nervous laughter. She straightened her jacket as Brady attempted to straighten his own.

"You okay?" he asked quietly.

She nodded. "As I'll ever be. Go ahead." She motioned for him to move away from the door and let her partner in.

Gina all but stumbled through the suddenly open doorway. She spied Erin first, a frown creasing her forehead. "What is going on with—" Then she spied Brady. "You," she finished, but her frown was immediately replaced by a delighted grin. "Well, I'll just let myself right back out."

"No, that won't be necessary," Brady said, trying to sound more terse than hoarse. Regardless, it gave Erin a shiver of remembered pleasure. "I was just leaving."

Gina winked at him. "If I'd waited a few more minutes, it might have been just the opposite. I'm so sorry."

"Gina!"

But Brady just chuckled and saluted her on his way out the door. He sent Erin a sizzling look over Gina's head, then he was gone.

Gina closed the door behind him then pressed her back against it. "Details. All of them. Slowly. Possibly twice."

Erin quickly busied herself with settling behind her desk once more and returning her attention where it should have been all along—on her computer screen.

"If you think I'm leaving with no juicy details," Gina warned playfully, "think again."

"I have to get this press release done before my meeting later with the mayor and Todd."

"Todd?"

"Fletcher. Henley's campaign manager. I've talked about him before."

"Yeah, but this is the first time you've called him by a name that can be repeated in mixed company. I didn't recognize it."

Erin laughed. "Hey, I just call 'em like I see 'em."

Gina crossed the room and propped a curvy hip on Erin's desk. "So, I bet he's a great kisser."

Erin didn't look up from her screen. "Todd Fletcher? I would have no idea. And I have no plans to find out."

"Ha ha, very funny. You know who I'm talking about."

Erin looked up with a knowing smile on her face. "And you're the only one doing the talking, or hadn't you noticed?"

Gina pulled a pout. "So you're really not going to tell me anything?"

"I'm really not. What is it you wanted?"

Gina paused, then laughed and shook her head. "I have no idea now. I took one look at your face, then his, and it went right out of my head."

"Well, if it comes back in your head, let me know. In the meantime, shoo. I'm really behind now." Erin followed that with a pointed look. "And this wasn't anything more than a temporary moment of insanity, so don't start some kind of campaign."

Sighing heavily, Gina slid off the desk, but her expression turned decidedly thoughtful as she crossed the room. She paused at the door. "Just tell me one thing."

Erin groaned and looked over the top of her monitor. "Then you'll promise never to mention this again?"

Gina just grinned. "I never make promises I can't keep, but it will get me out of your hair for now."

Erin rolled her eyes. "Okay, okay, what?"

"Kaboom?"

Erin was going to shake her head no, if for no other reason than to squash this right now. She had no idea what was going to happen next with Brady, but she didn't want to discuss it with Gina. Not yet anyway. She'd wait until she'd had at least a couple sleepless nights and had become truly neurotic about it. Then she'd call Gina. That's what girlfriends did.

But she couldn't lie. Her body wouldn't let her. It was already sighing in remembered rapture. So she gave it up, realizing the smile on her face had probably already given her away anyway. "Oh yeah," she said. "Major kaboom."

Gina started to rush the desk, her expression promising a barrage of questions, but Erin held up her hand. "No, you promised. Just one question. I answered it. Now go."

Gina stopped, but her expression turned mutinous. "I didn't think you were this cruel."

Erin laughed. "And I didn't think you were this hard up for salacious details. Has it been that long since your last hot date?"

Gina rolled her eyes. "I wouldn't know a hot date from a cold one lately."

Erin knew they'd both been more focused on work lately. She considered her best friend. "Maybe what we need is a girls' night out. We haven't taken time off in forever."

Gina considered the idea, then shook her head. "That sounds fine and all. But kind of pathetic in regards to our current conversation. What we really need is to get laid." Erin choked on a laugh, but Gina pushed on. "A good, long, headboard-banging all-nighter." Then she shot Erin a knowing look. "You know, it's a real shame to let all that prime detective go to waste. At least one of us should get what she needs."

Erin realized she'd been neatly trapped, but she wasn't going to let Gina take any satisfaction in it. She shrugged lightly instead. "Go right ahead. You could probably catch him down at the precinct right now."

Gina didn't buy the challenge for a second. She folded her arms at her waist and said, "Uh-huh. I take one step in his direction and I'm going to have spiked-heel prints permanently imprinted in my back as you race over me to get to him first."

"I absolutely refuse to respond to that on the grounds that it will incriminate me."

Satisfied now, Gina nodded. "Glad to see you've come to your senses. So finish that press release already and go round Detective Hunk up and herd him home." She opened the door, then leaned theatrically against the frame. "At least one of us will wake up smiling."

Erin snorted. "Yeah, right. I happen to know just how many pages are filled up in that little red book of yours. Starred ratings and all. So don't tell me how lonely you are. You're only lonely because you choose to be."

"You know, I admit I enjoy my rather footloose lifestyle when it comes to the opposite sex. It suits me right now." She waggled her eyebrows and added, "Even if I haven't had anything in a suit in weeks." Her expression sobered. "But can you honestly say the same, Erin? I know you are focused on this business, just like I am. But...I worry about you sometimes. You just don't handle those kind of jump-n-run relationships like I do."

Erin wanted to be insulted, but Gina knew her better than anyone. And she happened to be right. "Well, maybe I'll surprise you. And myself. Brady isn't looking for long-term, and I honestly can't right now. Besides, no way do I want to settle down with a cop. So..." She trailed off, not sure where she was going with this.

"So?" Gina urged. "So you're telling me there *is* more to this moment of insanity. Or you want there to be."

Erin shrugged, but quickly added, "I don't know if anything will happen, Gina. I—I have to think about this."

"See, that's half your problem. If you're in for the jump-n-run, you can't waste time thinking it to death. Takes all the thrill out. As long as you both know up front what the deal is, you just enjoy. That's the beauty of it. No worries, no strings, just a good time until it stops being good."

"Then what?"

"You just say thanks and move on."

"Just like that?"

"Just like that."

"And you're telling me your feelings don't get hurt?"

Gina laughed. "Who said I'm not the one saying goodbye first?"

"Is that your trick then?"

"I wouldn't call it a trick. But women are usually a bit more in tune to things than men are. I can usually tell if it's getting emotional and walk away. Usually, though, it just starts to bore me."

Erin couldn't ever imagine Brady ever boring her. But she could imagine getting tired of his job and the constant havoc it would likely cause with their attempts to find time together. Most likely that would be what finished them.

"Wheels are turning in there," Gina murmured. "You worried you might get emotional with our Detective Hunk?"

Erin snapped out of her reverie. "No. No, not at all." It was a good answer, and honest as far as she knew. So why was she still thinking it out? "He's far too intense and job-oriented. Police work is his whole life."

"So where do you fit in?"

Erin fought a smile as she recalled how she'd outlined her oh-so-practical plan to Brady. "A release valve. That's what we are for each other." She looked at her friend. "Everyone should have a release valve, right?"

"You won't get an argument from me." But she wasn't smiling. "Just be careful here, Erin."

"Now wait a minute. One second you're all but throwing me at him. 'Kaboom doesn't happen too often,' I believe were your exact words. Now you're warning me off. Make up your mind."

She just shrugged. "I guess I've thought more about it. And like I said earlier, I'm not sure you can handle the jump-n-run type relationship. I just don't want the kaboom to be your heart exploding into a million pieces."

"Never happen. Certainly not with Brady."

Gina studied her, then nodded. "If you really believe that, then you have my complete and total blessing." She grinned and saluted. "Welcome to the Jump Club."

Erin smiled dryly. "Gee, thanks. I think."

"Just remember, not too much thinking. That's what will get you into trouble. Just jump."

Erin said nothing as her best friend exited the room. "And then run like hell," she murmured.

She looked back at her computer, but her attention had strayed so far from work there was no getting back to it. Might as well go grab something to eat before her meeting with Henley and Fletcher.

Suddenly pizza and a beer sounded very good.

And just maybe she'd put a call in on her cell phone to Brady on the way over to Jimmy's. No thinking, Gina had said. Just do it.

She stood and straightened her hopelessly wrinkled suit. She'd have to change before going to city hall. She scooped up her purse and headed for the door. She'd stop by her place first.

No thinking, just do it. Gina's advice kept running

through her head. Which she totally blamed for the following idea that raced right behind it.

Maybe Jimmy's had takeout and they could eat at her place. After all, if she had to take her clothes off anyway... Erin swallowed hard, clutched her cell phone and got in the elevator.

8

BRADY BEGAN GOING over the report for the tenth time but the words refused to unblur. He needed coffee. No, the last thing he needed was more coffee. What he needed was some uninterrupted time in the sack. He groaned, then swore under his breath at the images that thought pumped right into his head. Like he needed any additional help thinking about what had happened earlier today in Erin's office.

Dear Lord, but the woman was sin in high heels. He couldn't recall ever feeling that blistered by one simple kiss. Not that there had been anything simple about that kiss. He shook his head, then rubbed his eyes. No, nothing simple about any aspect of anything having to do with Erin Mahoney. He should be sending thank-you flowers to her partner for interrupting them when she had. God only knows where that encounter would have ended up, but he was pretty damn certain one or both of them would have been naked before it was all said and done.

Which brought him to the reason he couldn't interpret one single word of the report in front of him. Was it all said and done? Would Erin realize that the two of them should never have played with fire? Especially not one as intense as this one could turn out to be.

Or would she expect to pick up where they'd so abruptly been forced to leave off?

And if so, what in the hell was his position on the matter?

"Position." Cradling his head in his hands, he groaned. He could think of any number of likely positions he'd enjoy getting into with Erin. His phone rang. "Thank you whoever you are," he murmured, then snatched up the receiver on the second ring. "O'Keefe. Homicide."

There was a clearing of a throat, then, "Brady?"

He let his forehead drop until it hit the report on his desk. "Erin."

There was a pause, as if she was trying to gauge his mood from that one single word. He wished her luck, since he had no idea what his mood was. Not precisely anyway. Frustrated, tired, cranky. Incredibly aroused. Damn, just hearing his name had him growing in his pants.

"I, um, well." She broke off and he actually fought a smile.

She was stuttering. Suddenly feeling better, he sat up. "I, um, well, what?" he asked, not bothering to hide his amusement.

"Are you hungry?" The question came out quickly, almost tersely.

He barely swallowed the groan. Hungry? He felt like a starving man at the moment. And it had nothing whatsoever to do with missing dinner. "Why?" It seemed the safest response. If there was such a thing around her.

"I haven't eaten yet and I have a meeting with Henley and his campaign guy later, so I—"

"You want me to go to dinner with you and the mayor?"

She laughed, suddenly sounding far more like the Erin who had all but crawled up his body in her office today.

"No, I don't want you to eat dinner with us. I'm not dining with Henley." There was a slight pause, then, "I thought you might like to grab something at Jimmy's and...you know...talk." Another pause which he did nothing to fill. "About...today. And tomorrow."

"Tomorrow? What's happening tomorrow?"

He could hear the sensuality in her voice as she answered. "That's what I want to talk about."

"Ah." Amazing how much a person could pack into one syllable, he thought.

"Yeah. Ah."

He delayed his response—mostly because he hadn't a clue what to say to that—just long enough for her to get her bearing first.

"I guess what I'm asking is if you want there to be a tomorrow. But I really don't want to talk about this on my cell phone. Have you eaten? You feel like Jimmy's?"

"No, I haven't eaten."

He heard her audible sigh of relief. So she wasn't all that sure of herself after all. Hmm.

"Twenty minutes? I have to go home and change clothes first."

"For Jimmy's?"

"No, for my meeting with Henley. I'm a bit...wrinkled."

Right. And he recalled in vivid detail just how he'd put those wrinkles in that designer fit-me-like-a-glove suit she'd been wearing today. Immediately after those details, his fevered imagination happily continued the scenario all the way to her standing in front of her closet climbing out of those wrinkled clothes.

"Brady?"

He jerked slightly and sat up straighter. "Yeah, I'm here. What time?"

"Twenty minutes?"

Right, she'd just said that, hadn't she. Maybe this wasn't a good idea. He had a ton of work to do. And not a snowball's chance in hell of getting through it now, he realized. If he thought his mind had gone on vacation after that little two-minute interlude earlier, it was on full hiatus now that she'd made it clear she still considered the situation between them a viable one.

"Yeah," he said gruffly. "Twenty minutes."

BRADY WALKED into Jimmy's like a man about to go before a firing squad. Which made no sense at all. Erin was bright, attractive, very easy to look at. And she was hot for his body. Any other man would be all but dancing into the pizza joint. But Brady wasn't any other man. Dammit.

The only thing that kept him remotely on an even keel was the recollection of her voice on the phone. Hesitant, unsure, almost shy. But it was enough to tell him she was as uncertain of this new path they were contemplating as he was. Which was why he'd decided on the way over here that, despite his willingness earlier, his answer was going to be no thank you. Albeit a very regretful no thank you.

If both of their instincts were clamoring for them to think twice, then he was going to damn well listen to the clamor for the both of them.

Erin was at the counter with the boys, watching a hockey game and sipping a beer. Her legs were so long she could cross them and still have enough left over to tuck one ankle behind the other. Perched on that bar stool, all that entwined length was damn sexy. And all he could think about was how beautifully those legs could entwine around him.

He strode over to the counter. "Hey."

She waved him silent for a moment, then let out a very unladylike holler when the Islanders' goalie let one by him, giving the Flyers a one point lead.

He found himself smiling at her easy camaraderie in a typically male milieu. Here he was all prepared to do battle like a gladiator...and she was more interested in hockey. He wasn't sure if he should be insulted, but he did relax a bit. Maybe this wouldn't be so hard. Maybe she'd already come to the same conclusion he had.

"I thought you were a football fan," he said.

She turned to him, her smile brilliant. "I am. I'm also a hockey fan. I also cheer on the 76ers."

"You forgot the Phillies."

"Baseball?" She made a face. "Never got into it."

"What, not brutal enough?"

She grinned. "Just not fast-paced enough for me."

He recalled that she had been an only girl with a number of brothers. That was where she'd learned all her commando moves when they were kids. It had likely been for her own survival. It was just his luck she'd done most of her practicing on him. "You want to watch the rest of the game?"

She shook her head. "No. Boucher has it sewn up. He's not letting anything by him tonight. Right, guys?"

As one they all turned toward her and nodded, glowing smiles on their faces. Brady thought for sure they were going to drop off their stools and genuflect at her high-heeled feet at any second.

"Come on," he said, "there's a table over there." He motioned to one in the far corner, farthest from the door and from her adoring fan club. Even Miller was hurrying to put a napkin under her mug before handing it to her.

"Here ya go, Erin," he said, his eyes crinkling at the corners.

Brady snorted. "Come on, before they make a sash out of coasters and proclaim you Ms. Jimmy's."

Erin merely rolled her eyes, said thanks to Miller and led the way to the corner table.

Once they were seated, facing each other, staring at one another, Brady wondered what he'd been in such an all-fired hurry for. He stared past Erin's shoulder at the men at the counter, thankful when Philly scored again and drew their attention back to the game.

"What do you want on your pizza?" She didn't bother looking at the menu.

A woman who knew what she wanted. He shouldn't

have been surprised. "You pick. You know I like everything."

She lifted one eyebrow. "Do you? I would have guessed you for a more selective type."

Brady sighed. "Okay, no double entendres. This is going to be difficult enough as it is."

Her smile faltered. "Difficult?" Then her expression smoothed. "Oh. I see." She ran her fingers over the chilled glass of her mug. "Why didn't you just tell me this on the phone?" She looked up at him, her smile smooth enough, as long as you didn't notice that it didn't reach her eyes. "I could have watched the game."

"Because I didn't decide until I was on my way over here."

Miller signaled from the counter for their order and Erin merely stared at Brady.

He relented with a sigh. "I guess we might as well eat."

Erin laughed, but there was little real humor in it. "Please, stop, you're making me feel so desirable."

"Sorry." Brady called to Miller to bring them one with the works. "No anchovies," he added.

"Thank you for that, at least."

He looked back at her, but his responding grin faded quickly. "Look, I'm sorry. This is probably not the place for us to have this conversation anyway."

She looked around, then back at him. "Where do you usually do the dump-n-run?"

"The dump-n— Excuse me?"

"Gina's term. For the end of the jump-n-run. Except I never even got to the jump part."

Brady didn't even pretend to know what the hell she was talking about. All his carefully rehearsed lines had already become a half-forgotten jumble. "I figured if we were both so unsure about this arrangement, it was probably a good idea to listen to those second thoughts."

"Why?"

He stared at her. "Why?"

She nodded. "Of course we're going to have second thoughts and probably third ones. I would no matter who I was contemplating beginning a – Whatever it is we're beginning."

"See? That right there is why we shouldn't be beginning anything. We can't even describe what it is we're beginning."

"The way I see it, maybe that just proves we're being smart about the whole thing. Maybe it's when you jump right in and don't think it out first that trouble happens."

"So what exactly are you saying?"

"I'm saying we should discuss it."

"Discuss it." Brady shook his head. "Like this is some kind of business merger."

Her mouth curved. "Well, a merger anyway."

Brady felt his neck heat up. Damn but it was hard to say no to her when she smiled at him like that. "Maybe there is a reason people don't discuss it," he said evenly. "Because it's not supposed to be coldly outlined and signed on the dotted line, like a deal to be closed that sort of takes the fun out of it, don't you think?"

She set her mug down and leaned forward on her elbows. "I don't think we'd have any trouble whatsoever making this fun."

Brady's throat tightened. As did other parts of his body.

"Spontaneity is for people interested in romance and building real relationships," she went on. "I don't think that's what we want here, so why should there be any pretense?"

Brady chuckled. "Listen to you. You sound like most men in situations like this."

"Then I should be your fantasy come true. A woman who wants nothing more than to spend some downtime with you. No demands, no relationship other than two people letting off steam. Together."

Brady was saved from responding to that immediately when their pizza arrived. "Thanks, Miller."

The older man nodded, but his eyes never left Erin. As he turned to head back to the counter, he winked at Brady and made the okay sign where Erin couldn't see him. Brady shook his head and wondered just what he was he doing here anyway?

He looked back at Erin in time to see her roll a long string of melted cheese around her tongue, then close her eyes as she pulled it into her mouth to savor it.

Okay, so that was why he was here. She was sexy, willing and totally up front about her reasons for wanting him. Which brought up another question. "Why me?"

Her eyes blinked open and she swallowed her bite in one lump. After chasing it down with a sip of beer, she said, "What do you mean?"

"Exactly what I said. Why me? You must have plenty of other corporate types in your life that would be more than willing to agree to...an arrangement like this."

She narrowed her eyes. "I'm not sure I like the way you phrased that."

Now it was Brady who propped his elbows on the table. "And how else would you phrase it? You were the one who said this wasn't about hearts and flowers. So if it's going to be an affair, why not call it that?"

Erin held his gaze with her own mutinous one for several long seconds before finally looking away. "I guess you're right."

"Unless you're saying this isn't really just a release-valve kind of thing and underneath what you really want is the hearts and flowers."

Her response to that was as immediate as it was obviously sincere. "With you?" She snorted. "I don't think so."

"Gee, good thing my ego isn't easily bruised."

She laughed. "Sorry. But, to answer your earlier question, that is why you're perfect for this. I don't really want to get into anything serious in my life right now. And it seems that all those corporate suits you mentioned never seem content to leave things casual. I don't want to be having to relate my every move to someone else, or schedule my life around someone else's expectations of where I should be and what I should be doing. You made it very clear the other day that this was exactly how you felt, too. But just because we're focused on our own lives and careers doesn't mean we don't get a little needy from time to time." She looked him directly in the eye. "So I figured we'd match up well. You certainly can't argue that the chemistry is there."

No, he couldn't, but something about all this bothered him. "So you had this all laid out, just waiting for the right guy?"

"Of course not, that's not how I meant it at all. I never even thought about having—"

"An affair?"

She ground her teeth, but her eyes held some amusement. "That sounds tawdry, like something people do that they're not supposed to be doing, with someone they're not supposed to be doing it with. You and I are free agents here. Surely there's a better word for it than that."

Brady was smiling now too. He enjoyed several bites of his pizza and let her stew for a bit. She was really something else. Trying so hard to be all cosmopolitan about the idea and at the same time obviously struggling with it. "Like I said, if we can't even comfortably describe this, maybe there should be no this."

Erin put her pizza back on her plate. "You know, maybe you're right."

Her surprise turnabout made him pause. What, was he upset now that she'd seen his point? How perverse was that? Was he really hoping she'd persuade him to agree to her plan?

She glanced at her watch and swore softly under her breath. "I have to go." She looked at him, then offered a slight smile. "Well, can't blame a girl for trying, right?"

Brady shrugged, wondering just how bad a mistake he was making here. She was right. Her offer was every man's fantasy. He couldn't believe he was letting her walk away. But he was. He hated being the good guy.

She gathered her purse and the bill and stood.

"I'll get that," Brady said, reaching for the ticket.

She shook her head. "It was my invite. Just enjoy the rest of it, okay?"

He started to argue, then realized she was trying hard to save face. Had this encounter really been that difficult for her? Apparently so. He was oddly touched by that. That she'd stepped that far out of her comfort zone because she'd thought her idea might work. He realized then that for all of Erin's apparent ease with her sexuality, she was hardly free in sharing it. He wished he had the words to tell her that it was flattering to him that she'd offered in the first place.

As she moved beside where he was seated on her way out, he placed his hand on her arm, stopping her. "I didn't make the decision easily."

She said nothing, simply holding his gaze. Finally she smiled. "Thanks for that, O'Keefe."

O'Keefe. He guessed he deserved the return to formality. He couldn't have it both ways. "Yeah. No problem."

"When will you have another update on the case for me? For Henley, I mean."

Business. That's all that was going to be between them now. He sighed, unable to escape the feeling that he'd just really blown it. "In a few days. I'll let you know."

"Fine. The poll figures are worrying. I'm going to push the mayor, or should I say Fletcher, to let me come up with something on this. Dodging things like he has is only going to work for so long. Too much more and it's going to come back on him. Any help from you would be greatly appreciated."

"Sure."

His easy acquiescence had her raising an eyebrow. "What, you're feeling sorry for me now?" But rather than look honestly chagrined, she smiled. "If we're not going to tussle in bed together, at least give me a good tussle otherwise, okay, O'Keefe?" And then she paid the tab, said goodbye to her cheering section and sailed out the door without another glance in his direction.

Good thing Brady hadn't been chewing on pizza. He'd have choked on it after her parting shot. Had he really thought she'd been uncomfortable with this whole thing? You'd never know it by the way she left.

But as he lingered over another piece of pizza and the rest of his beer, he kept picturing her expression and recalling the hint of uncertainty in her voice as they'd talked it over. Erin might put on a good show— and it was a hell of a good one—but beneath all her considerable God-given attributes and clever intellect she was just as insecure as anyone else.

And damn but she'd have been great to tussle in the sheets with. Brady downed the rest of his beer in one pull and stood. He was an idiot. He waved goodbye to Miller and pushed out the door.

But he remained an unattached idiot, and that was all that mattered in the end.

9

ERIN'S MIND was definitely not on business as she entered city hall. It was still back in Jimmy's. With Brady. She cringed inwardly as she recalled their conversation. He'd turned her down. Flat.

She felt like a total fool. But then she'd remember that kiss in her office. He'd been more than willing then. She couldn't help wondering what would have happened if Gina hadn't interrupted when she did. Would Brady have stopped them? She wasn't so sure. And if they'd ended up...more satisfied...would he have still been so willing to write off her idea?

She stepped off the elevator, trying hard to get her mind off her personal life and back on her business life, when Todd Fletcher stepped forward. She almost ran smack into him before she noticed he'd been waiting by the doors. For her? She immediately checked her watch. "Hi. I'm not late, am I?"

Todd took her elbow and steered her around the corner, away from the mayor's office. "No. We have to talk."

Frowning, Erin extricated her elbow and stopped. "Talk about what?"

It was obvious Todd was agitated, but then that was pretty much the general state of the mayor's campaign

The Harlequin Reader Service® — Here's how it works:

Accepting your 2 free books and gift places you under no obligation to buy anything. You may keep the books and gift and return the shipping statement marked "cancel." If you do not cancel, about a month later we'll send you 4 additional novels and bill you just $3.34 each in the U.S., or $3.80 each in Canada, plus 25¢ shipping & handling per book and applicable taxes if any.* That's the complete price and   compared to cover prices of $3.99 each in the U.S. and $4.50 each In Canada — it's quite a bargain! You may cancel at any time, but if you choose to continue, every month we'll send you 4 more books, which you may either purchase at the discount price or return to us and cancel your subscription.

*Terms and prices subject to change without notice. Sales tax applicable in N.Y. Canadian residents will be charged applicable provincial taxes and GST.

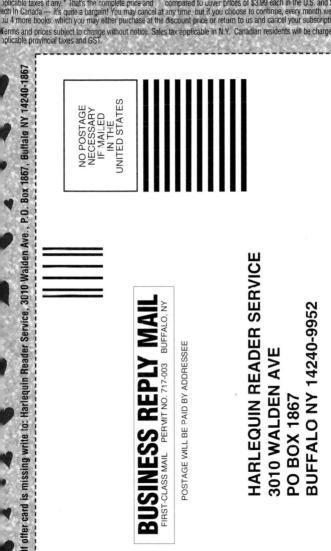

If offer card is missing write to: Harlequin Reader Service, 3010 Walden Ave., P.O. Box 1867, Buffalo NY 14240-1867

NO POSTAGE
NECESSARY
IF MAILED
IN THE
UNITED STATES

BUSINESS REPLY MAIL

FIRST-CLASS MAIL   PERMIT NO. 717-003   BUFFALO, NY

POSTAGE WILL BE PAID BY ADDRESSEE

HARLEQUIN READER SERVICE
3010 WALDEN AVE
PO BOX 1867
BUFFALO NY 14240-9952

manager. Only she quickly realized he was beyond his normal agitation and had moved somewhere in the vicinity of fury.

"What in the world is wrong?" she demanded. "Has something happened with the mayor?"

"Don't act all innocent with me. I knew hiring you was a bad idea from the beginning. I told the mayor I could manage this little glitch with Sanderson, but he thought keeping this separate from the campaign committee was a good idea."

"Little glitch? *Little?*" Erin laughed derisively. She'd known Todd wasn't keen on her involvement with the mayor, that he'd felt threatened by her, but he'd sulked in silence for the most part. Until now apparently. "I don't think I'd characterize Henley's single biggest campaign contributor, one of his most vocal supporters, the self-proclaimed moral leader of his party, being found dead in a satin tutu as a *little* problem, Todd." She propped a hand on her hip. "And the fact that he hired me tells me he didn't think so either."

"For all the good it's done him."

"Because he isn't taking *my* advice." She sent him a pointed look.

"Maybe that's because he suspects you aren't telling him everything. What's going on between you and the detective?"

He'd caught her so off guard she didn't have time to mask her surprise. "Just what the hell are you insinuating?"

"I'm saying you're getting awfully cozy with

O'Keefe and I'm not seeing it translate to help for the mayor. So I want to know who you're helping here?"

"First of all, I'm doing what the mayor is asking of me, which is assisting you. Despite my advice to the contrary. I think he should be taking a more active role in responding to the outcry over Sanderson's death." Her gaze narrowed. "I'm sure his refusal has more to do with you than with his own feelings on the matter."

Todd opened his mouth to respond, but the look in his eyes was all she needed to see. "Secondly, what I do on my own time, and with whom, is my business."

"So it's just coincidence that you're seeing the lead detective on the case socially?"

Erin's fingers tightened on the handle of her briefcase. "Who says we're seeing each other socially?"

Todd shrugged now, but the smirk was still there. "I have sources."

"I'm still in the dark over the problem here. Even if I were seeing Detective O'Keefe socially, I don't see the conflict. If anything, I was told by both the mayor and the commissioner to get close to him."

"As it pertains to the murder investigation. Or is that the only way you know how to go about collecting information? On your back?"

Erin had never punched anyone. At least not since becoming an adult. But her childhood survival instincts, honed to a razor sharp edge by being raised with a fistful of brothers, were kicking in. However, maturity had brought a few weapons of its own. And it was those she turned to now.

She dropped her defensive stance and allowed a siren smile to curve her lips. "Now, Todd, we both know I'm quite capable of getting information without ever resorting to taking my clothes off." She moved closer, gratified when she saw his eyes widen and his throat visibly work. "I mean, I have nothing against sex, but let's be honest. I think we both know I don't need to use that to get what I want." Small beads of sweat popped out on his pale forehead. "Agreed?"

Todd jerked his glance downward, but said nothing.

"Now," she went on, voice as smooth as silk, "I don't know what your little eyes and ears told you, but if I have any information I think will help the mayor, then I'll be the first one to tell him." She dipped her chin slightly and dragged his focus off her breasts. He flushed hotly as her smile grew. "Do we have an understanding? Todd?"

He only scowled. "You don't belong here."

Erin didn't respond, but merely stepped around him, her smile instantly fading to a snarl as she walked to the mayor's office. What a jerkface. Of course, she knew this wouldn't be the end of it.

She would have to get Henley to agree to see her privately, away from Todd's influence, and try to talk some sense into him. He was paying her good money to do a job that Todd was undermining every step of the way. It didn't have to be this way. All she had to do was get some time alone to explain and defend her strategy. She also made a note to call Brady and tell him he still had someone looking over his shoulder. One of Todd's weasels. "It takes one to know one," she muttered.

She pushed into the office, smiled at Henley's receptionist, then motioned her to remain at her desk. "I'll let myself in." Todd would be right on her heels, so she wanted to get at least a minute with Henley first to arrange that appointment.

"Hello, Erin," the mayor greeted her warmly, rising from his chair. "Sorry to have this meeting so late in the day, but you know how it is."

She laughed lightly, as she was expected to. "A politician's work is never done." She approached his desk. "Sir, if I may, I'd like to schedule some time with you alone, to go over the proposals that I—"

His welcoming smile faded to a resigned look that didn't bode well for her. "Erin, we've discussed this and I already told you that Todd and I—"

"Sir, I understand Todd's reservations about you taking a more vocal role in the investigation into Sanderson's death. That first press conference was horrible, no question. But the initial furor is dying down and now the media are hounding the police for clues and even doing investigative work on their own. I really feel now is the time for us to step forward and—"

Todd entered the room behind her. "Erin, unless you have any new information that conclusively gives us an edge with the voting constituency, I really feel keeping the mayor on the present track is the right thing to do. His poll numbers have evened out and I'm confident of an eventual upswing."

Erin swallowed the urge to stick her tongue out at him. The little creep had rebounded faster than she'd expected. She also understood his unspoken threat regarding information from Brady. She had no doubt Todd planned to use whatever he thought he knew about her and Brady to discredit her further with the mayor. And while she knew she'd have no problem refuting his nasty innuendo, she also realized she was tired of all this petty bullshit.

She kept her attention firmly on Henley and pretended Todd wasn't even there. "We need to make a firm commitment to seeing the investigation through. We know it was murder now, so discounting the manner in which Sanderson was found will be somewhat easier in terms of how it affects you, and more importantly, the city. You need to show the people that you are outraged at what was done to him and that you won't rest until the murderer is caught. I think—"

"I think we need to spend our time here more wisely," Todd said smoothly, sweeping in front of her. "I have the schedule for your radio spots all mapped out, Mayor. Why don't we go to the conference room and look over the guidelines?"

Henley, weak-spined animal that she'd learned he was, looked at Erin with an expression that was as good as an apologetic shrug. She knew right then that the only reason Henley kept her on was because he hadn't figured out how to fire her. How someone so muddled and softhearted had become mayor she had no idea. She probably didn't have to look much further than Todd. Which spelled out certain doom for any hope she had of working effectively for the mayor now. Likely it had been Commissioner Douglas who had pushed him to hire her in the first place. She didn't see Henley having that kind of independent thinking. Not with Todd hovering.

"Come on," Henley said with his charismatic "let's all get along" smile that had won the hearts of voters everywhere.

It hadn't won hers.

"I'll get Teri to make us some coffee." Smiling oh so congenially, he stretched out his arm, indicating she was to precede him to the conference room. "Have you eaten?"

Todd's swift smile in her direction told her he knew of this evening's meal with Brady. She'd wondered, now she knew. Worm. "Yes, I have, thanks."

Rather than follow Henley's direction, however, she paused in front of him, swiftly debated the words on the edge of her tongue, then went with her instincts and turned to face him. "Sir, if I may take a moment."

He lifted a questioning eyebrow.

She purposely kept her gaze off Todd, knowing he'd be all but preening in victory. However, as much as it grated, she knew when to fold. "I appreciate that you hired my firm to help you through such a difficult time. I only wish we could have been of greater service."

His politician's smile faded to uncertainty. "What exactly are you saying?"

"Perhaps you don't require my help at this point. Todd feels he is doing fine overseeing your campaign and you have made the choice to make that your priority." Her stomach knotted up. Was she actually doing this? Walking away from their biggest client to date? Gina was going to kill her. "I simply feel that my services are redundant here and that perhaps the fee you are paying us would be better served funding other aspects of your reelection campaign."

She wanted to gag on her political correctness. But she wasn't in business to make enemies of past clients. Not if she wanted to stay in business.

Henley studied her as if she were speaking a foreign language. Of course, in a way, she was. She was pretty certain no one had ever walked away from a lucrative position such as this without being fired or dismissed first. But it was evident her work here was as done as it would ever be.

"I see." As predicted, he looked to Todd, who could barely contain his glee. "With this investigation into Morton's death still in the early stages, do you think it wise to end our association with Erin's firm? I don't want to give the wrong impression. After all, she's done her best."

Erin ground her teeth as Todd appeared to give his query some serious thought. When he glanced snottily at her, however, she allowed her face to slide into the same knowing smile she'd put on out in the hallway. At least she got the very slim satisfaction of seeing his self-satisfied expression falter, even if only for a moment. He reached up to loosen his tie, carefully averting his gaze from that point on. It was a small victory, but she'd take them where she could get them.

"Mayor," he said, trying to sound mournful. "I understand your concerns, but you know we've taken the strong position of trusting our police force and the commissioner to handle this thing quickly. We've made that commitment work for you with the public and I think that is the way to go with this. In that respect, I think it was very wise of Ms. Mahoney here to realize her role in this incident has come to an end."

Erin looked at the two of them and swallowed the bitter taste of defeat. Between these two and what had happened with Brady today, her opinion of men at the moment was at an all-time low. She didn't care. She simply wanted out of here. It was going to be hard enough to tell Gina.

She also realized she'd just severed her only continuing link to Brady. And that made her pause. Was that why she'd really done this?

No. No, she'd known for some time this was coming. It just took Todd's snarky little comments to make her realize the time was now. At least this way she'd controlled her exit, but then, wasn't that what she did for a living? Put the best spin on a bad situation? She also realized that under Todd's direction, it was very likely this investigation would sooner rather than later come back to bite the mayor's backside. And she would rather not be the one responsible for covering those teeth marks when the time came. She'd much rather let Todd contend with that.

The satisfaction that prospect gave her enabled her to turn to face the weasel. She extended her hand, her smile bright and hard. "I wish you the best of luck with the campaign." *You're going to need it*, she silently messaged. Then she turned back to the mayor, all business now. "I'm certain your office can handle our final billing. Best of luck in the election, sir." She shook his hand. She shouldn't have been surprised by the level of relief she felt as she turned around and walked back out of the office. She said goodbye to a surprised Teri and walked out of city hall.

If any other politicians wanted their services, she was directing them to Gina.

She thought about going by the office on the off chance Gina was still there, but decided against it. She was wiped out, both emotionally and physically. Erin wanted to make sure her partner heard the news straight from her, but she could call Gina from home. That way she could deliver the news with a glass of wine in her hand.

She flashed back to the beer she'd had earlier with Brady. That meeting hadn't gone as hoped either. "Not exactly your best day," she murmured as she headed home.

Pulling into her spot at her condo's underground parking garage, she realized it was going to get worse before it got better. Brady was waiting for her.

He stood silently by the elevator doors. He shouldn't look so good, she thought. Rumpled as usual, his tie was completely gone now. Five o'clock shadow shaded his strong jaw, but his eyes were as sharp as ever.

"What happened?" he said tersely.

"Hello yourself," she returned just as sharply. As much as she'd like to be up for this encounter—there was no denying seeing him had sent a rush of anticipation through her—she was done for the day. And that rush was another reason for her not to hang around down here. Getting turned down once was enough for today. "What are you doing here?"

"Why did Henley fire you?"

Her mouth dropped open, then snapped shut as her eyes narrowed. "That little snake," she muttered. Apparently Todd hadn't wasted any time getting the news out. "Is that what he told you?" She shook her head and let out a mirthless laugh. "I bet he couldn't wait to write that press release. He probably assured Henley he'd deal with it discreetly." She snorted, talking more to herself than to Brady. "Yeah, right. As discreetly as he's done everything else, including having me followed."

Brady took her arm as she went to push past him. "What?"

She stopped, but firmly extricated her arm. Having him touch her right now was only adding insult to injury. At least the way her body reacted to it made it feel that way. "You heard me. I really don't want to talk about this right now. But for the record, Detective, I was the one to end my business relationship with the mayor." If she'd been more on the ball, she would have headed straight to the office and composed her own press release. But her mind had been in a jumble. Maybe Brady had been right in turning her down. She needed to get her focus back.

She moved past him and all but felt him come up behind her. She stabbed at the elevator buttons. *Come on, doors, help me out here and let me make my exit.*

"Erin."

Apparently she wasn't going to get any breaks today. Brady barking at her was easy to push past. Brady saying her name all concerned like that turned her remaining defenses to mush. She sighed heavily, but didn't turn to look at him. "I really want to go upstairs and fix myself a drink. I have to call Gina." She swore under her breath, realizing she wouldn't put it past Todd to make a call to the office under pretense of getting the billing work done. Her partner might already know. Hopefully Gina would wait for an explanation from her before losing it.

Brady placed a gentle but firm hand on her shoulder and turned her to face him. "Why don't you let me take you out for that drink. I want to hear what happened."

"Why? It had nothing to do with you. I knew this was coming, but tonight I realized I had been rendered so ineffective by the mayor's own campaign manager that it was better to distance myself and my firm from the decisions he was making. Or should I say, decisions Todd the Weasel was making for him."

A small smile quirked the corners of his mouth, even his eyes crinkled a bit. "Is that your official response, Ms. Mahoney?" At her dry smile, his own smile grew. "There, that's more like it."

Erin stared at him, wondering why he was really here. Was he worried that her ending this job would somehow affect his investigation? She couldn't see how. So why? She was simply too tired to speculate.

"I appreciate the offer of a drink, but I really just want to go upstairs, get out of these heels and shove this entire day away."

Brady's smile dimmed a little. "I'm sorry for the part

that I played in making you want to shove the day away."

Truth be told, if he stood there much longer, looking like he did, smelling so good and so...male, she'd find it harder and harder to shove him away. She sighed. "I'm really not up to this right now, okay?"

He sighed too, then raked his hand through his already tousled hair. "Yeah, okay." He stepped back as the elevator doors finally slid open. "I do want to hear more about this. Will you call me tomorrow?"

She frowned. "Is there something you're not telling me here?"

He looked honestly surprised. "No. Why?"

"I'm only trying to figure out why you're being so insistent. I'm a big girl. My business won't crumble because I decided to let this client go. I already told you it had nothing to do with you. So—" She shrugged. "Why the dogged persistence? Did Todd say anything else? Is there some other rumor I should be aware of? Some nasty surprise awaiting me in the morning paper?"

Now it was Brady's turn to frown. "What would make you think that?" He stepped close again and the doors slid shut on the empty elevator behind her. "What exactly happened at city hall tonight? You said Todd has had you followed?"

Erin sighed, but realized that perhaps she should talk things out here and now. If for no other reason than to make sure Todd didn't have some other nefarious plan to discredit her. She'd assumed her ending her association with Henley was all he wanted, but maybe she was wrong. She didn't think so, but right now she wasn't exactly at her sharpest. "Okay, maybe we should talk about this." She shifted her feet and winced at the bite her shoes put on her toes. *Vanity, thy name is woman,* she thought ruefully.

Brady, sharp as ever, caught her little reaction. "Maybe we should. Would you mind if I came up? That way you could get off those towers of torture you call shoes, we could both have a much-needed drink and then I promise I'll get out of your hair."

She looked at him, then burst out laughing.

"What did I say that was so funny?"

That he looked more than a little hurt at her reaction to his offer only made her laugh harder. "I'm sorry." She managed to get herself under control, but her grin remained. "It's just that I spent the better part of today trying to figure out how to get you into my apartment and failed." Her mouth quirked. "Miserably I might add."

He had to smile. "Amazing how things work out, isn't it?"

"I should have figured it would be much easier if it were about business." Suddenly both of their smiles faded.

Brady might still be in her life, for the moment anyway. But he hadn't come here to take her to bed. She smiled lightly, hoping it reached her eyes. "I'm leaving all my feminine wiles on the doorstep, okay?"

His wry grin and nod should have been reassuring. "Whatever wiles I might have will be left there, too."

She decided there was something really pathetic

about having the man you intended to seduce come up to your apartment anyway for what amounted to a friend-to-friend chat. She supposed she should be thankful. Brady would be a good friend to have.

Only as he guided her into the elevator and turned to push the button, her gaze was drawn to the way his hair curled against his collar, the way his shoulders stretched the width of his jacket, even the way he punched the floor number with that strong, thick finger of his. Pathetic didn't even begin to cover it. Because, smart or otherwise, she still wanted to be a whole lot more than friends with Detective Brady O'Keefe.

10

It shouldn't have surprised Brady to discover that Erin's taste in décor was so sensual. She was, after all, a woman clearly comfortable with her own sensuality. Or at least, she certainly gave all appearances of it.

He followed her through the foyer into the living room. Deep jewel tones dominated throughout. One wall was painted a rich emerald green. The carpeting was a lush pale gold. It set off the oak furnishings as well as the green, heavily stuffed couch. Plump pillows of ruby, midnight blue and gold had been tossed in piles at both ends.

He looked around, realizing there was nothing lavish or even particularly expensive about the place. It was about par for someone up and coming in the world of business. And yet, he'd have described it as sumptuous. Even decadent. She'd made the most of what she had...and hadn't held herself back at all. This was definitely all Erin Mahoncy here.

"Very nice place," he said.

She had just kicked off her heels and punched the button to get her phone messages. She looked at him in surprise. "Thanks." She shrugged a bit self-consciously. "It's not very big, but it suits me."

He nodded and left her to retrieve her messages

while he glanced around. Tall bookshelves, crammed full of all kinds of books, both fiction and nonfiction, filled one wall. Watercolors of the city dotted one wall. Another was filled with a scattering of odd-size, framed photos of Erin, Gina and some of their more illustrious clients to date. He wandered around, smiling at the variety of her clientele. He doubted her job was ever boring.

The bar that separated the small kitchen from the living area held more photos, this time family and, he supposed, other friends of hers. He noticed a small stereo system tucked away in the corner with a few CDs scattered on top of it, gathering dust. However, the other corner was dominated by a large-screen, state-of-the-art television. He grinned. She could give or take music, but the lady liked her sports big, bright and in Dolby surround sound.

She was still listening to messages, frowning now. He looked past her to the small dining nook. The kitchen was wedged between the nook and where he stood now. Which meant the other two doors likely led to a bathroom...and a bedroom.

I'm leaving all my feminine wiles on the doorstep.

Her words echoed through his mind. A mind that was going to stay firmly on business. He doggedly returned his attention to the living room just as Erin was hanging up the phone and stabbing the rewind button on the answering machine. Her expression said it all.

"Gina heard, huh?"

Swearing softly, Erin nodded. "Lovely end to a

lovely day." She bent down to pick up her shoes. "Just lovely."

"You need to call her? I don't mind waiting. Just show me where the coffeemaker is and I'll be glad to make a pot."

Erin shot him a brief look of mock astonishment. "Cop coffee? Thanks, but I don't think I want you near my beans."

He smiled. "Hey, give me good beans, I can make good coffee. I can't help it if the station house buys Jim's Beans."

"Jim's Beans? Never heard of them."

"Jim means generic."

"Ah. Well, I was thinking more along the lines of an adult beverage. I have some white wine chilling in the fridge."

Brady made a face. "Girly drink."

Amused, Erin arched an eyebrow. "I see. Big bad cop like you definitely needs something more macho. Well, the beer is in the fridge, too." She motioned behind her. "Right through that door." Her tone shifted to that deeper, drier voice he so enjoyed. "And it's not Jim's Beer, either."

He grinned. "Lucky me."

She passed by him, close enough for him to get another whiff of the scent he'd been enjoying during their brief elevator ride. Spicy, earthy. Just like the woman wearing it. He watched her cross the room to the door he knew led to the bedroom. Where she would probably stand in front of her closet and strip just as he'd imagined earlier today, and was trying even harder not to think about now.

Too late.

It wasn't his fault. Not really. Women were all hung up on the boxers versus briefs thing, so a man couldn't be condemned for wondering panty hose...or just hose. And, therefore, garters...and garter belts. The question had simply popped into his mind. Perfectly normal thing to wonder about. And could he help it if the visual simply followed before he could stop it? No, of course not.

But could he stop thinking about it now that he'd realized where his mind was leading him?

No, of course not. He sighed and headed for the kitchen.

Maybe this had been a really bad idea after all. He'd heard about her ending her business relationship with the mayor. Actually, he'd heard it the other way around and that's why he'd come over. He'd dropped by her office first and it had been locked up and dark. So he'd come here and waited. She hadn't asked how he'd known where she lived, but being a cop, it hadn't been all that hard to find out. She'd probably figured that out, too. At least she hadn't been upset with him.

She also hadn't been spitting mad, which was how he'd expected to find her. One look at her face and he'd realized that the story coming out of the mayor's office had only emerged after someone had tinkered with it first.

Why did you come here?

Her question played through his mind again. He

would have sworn it was simply the cop instinct, wondering if something had gone wrong and if it affected his investigation. And even if he wasn't totally buying that, he had somehow made himself believe he might have also come as a friend.

A friend who'd realized he now had no reason to ever see her again since he'd stupidly tossed the release-valve plan back in her face. Not that he was here to see if she was still interested. No way. Once he'd realized she had controlled the end of the business liaison with Henley, he'd been fully prepared to leave her alone.

Bull hockey.

He ignored that. No, he'd only stayed because of that remark she'd made about Todd Fletcher having had her followed. And truthfully, he did have every intention of finding out what the hell that was all about.

He pulled a bottle of imported beer out of the fridge, nodding in respect for her taste. He spied the white wine and pulled that out as well. He opened a cabinet or two, didn't see any glassware and decided to stop and wait for her. And while he was at it, he might as well stop lying to himself, too. Sure, he was concerned about his investigation. And sure, he wanted to be Erin's friend.

But now that he was standing in her apartment, knowing full well she was less than twenty yards and one closed door away from him, skimming her silky hose down those dear-God-could-they-be-any-longer legs of hers... Well, he knew as well as he could ever know anything that there were issues a whole lot deeper than a police investigation and simple friendship that had him sipping beer and staring like a starved man at her bedroom door.

The only question that remained was how he was going to deal with that reality.

"Down the beer and run like hell," he muttered. Instead, he found himself picking up the remote off the end table. "You could run a space station with this thing." He pushed buttons until her Jumbotron of a television sizzled to life. The ESPN SportsCenter commentators blared into the living room. He tried to swallow the smile and couldn't. He found the flashback button and pressed that. ESPN2. Big surprise. He pushed it again and his eyes widened. Well, well. He'd expected Home Team Sports or CNN. But this was no sports or news channel. He found the menu button and skimmed down the list until he found the channel number. "The Romance Channel?"

His gaze darted to the closed door between them. "Who'd have thought it from Terror Mahoney?" Romance? Hearts and flowers and happy endings? Naw. Sure, she talked a good game of wanting to settle down and all. But that was future talk. Right now she was a woman who boldly talked about needing a release and searching for a valve—namely him. He'd have figured her interests for something hotter, like the female equivalent of the Playboy Channel. Did they have a Playgirl Channel?

He flicked the screen off. He was beginning to see firsthand just what a bundle of interesting contradictions she truly was. "None of which you'll be unraveling," he admonished himself. It wasn't up to him to reconcile her confident in-your-face sexy public persona with the far more private personal self that was underneath all the flash. Or the sports fanatic with a sentimental happily-ever-after streak running through her. That last part alone should have had him running for the nearest door. Only the door he kept looking at led to her bedroom.

Just then it opened and he swore he almost whined in disappointment when she emerged wearing faded jeans and a big baggy sweatshirt. What had he been hoping for? He silently snorted. What every red-blooded male hopes for, of course. Naughty lingerie.

And yet, as she moved toward him, he found himself just as turned on as if she'd been wearing a French corset. Maybe it was her bare feet, looking so cute and somehow vulnerable. Maybe it was the fresh face scrubbed clean of her professional warpaint, or the way her soft clothes still managed to showcase her long, lean curves.

Or maybe it was just her. Period. *Dangerous ground here, O'Keefe. Step lightly.*

"Sorry I took so long," she said. "I wanted to call Gina and set her straight."

"Is she okay?" His voice was a little hoarse. All that visualizing he'd been doing, most likely. He covered it with a long pull on his beer.

Erin was distracted enough that she didn't seem to notice. "She's not happy, but she understood. It's a good thing she won't be anywhere near Todd Fletcher in the near future." Her amusement didn't reach her eyes. "As much as I'd like to be ringside at that bout."

She looked tired, more tired than he'd realized, despite her protestations in the garage. Suddenly he felt very intrusive. *Why did you come here?* Good question. "I, uh, looked for some glasses, for your wine." He tried a smile. "I stopped just short of snooping, promise."

Her thoughts were a million miles away and it took her a moment to focus on him. *Well,* he thought wryly, *no need to worry that she's having any problem keeping her mind off their earlier conversation.* "Listen, it's late. Maybe we should put this off after all. I really didn't mean to barge my way in."

Her attention swung more fully to him. "Oh, you absolutely meant to barge your way in." Her dry smile resurfaced as she skirted past him and went into the small kitchen.

He wisely stayed on the other side of the bar in the living room. "Yeah, well, comes with the job, I guess."

"I guess," she agreed, setting a slender wineglass on the counter between them. "Although I can hardly point fingers. My job has been known to require a bit of barginess." She took a sip of her wine and Brady felt some part of himself tighten in response to watching her slender throat work.

"Can I get you another beer?" she asked, oblivious to his struggle.

He set his empty bottle on the counter. "No." The last thing he needed was any help impairing his already apparently impaired judgment. Perhaps if he got the conversation back to the reason he'd come up here in the first place. "So explain this thing about Fletcher having you followed. Why would he do that?"

He hated making her scowl, bringing the tension lines back to her forehead. But he had to know what was going on.

"Who knows why Todd does what he does? Information is power to someone like him and he likes to have as much of both as he can amass." She took another sip of wine and came around the counter, gesturing with her glass toward the couch as she continued. "I told you he was miffed that I was brought in to handle the Sanderson situation. More than miffed, actually."

"He thought he should have handled it? But he's the campaign guy, right? Henley doesn't want to mix with that."

She nodded and took a seat at one end of the couch. "Well, Todd saw this whole thing as a campaign issue, nothing more. I think Henley realized it was more than just a reelection situation, something that could potentially tarnish everything. Sanderson had been linked with him both personally and professionally for some time."

Brady debated remaining standing, but he felt bad enough for all but interrogating her in own home. He didn't need to loom over her while he did it. Friends didn't loom. So he sat. As far away as possible. "So he followed you for what purpose? Hoping to find some kind of dirt on you? I don't get it."

"He's been the one keeping Henley from taking my

advice, but he came up short on getting Henley to fire me altogether. I think the commissioner was instrumental in that. His influence on the mayor is strong."

"And vice versa," Brady muttered, but waved her on when she looked at him expectantly.

"Anyway, I guess he was trying to prove I wasn't doing my job. He knew you and I had dinner together and snagged me going into the meeting tonight on what I had found out about the investigation. He insinuated I had to get you in bed to get the information I needed."

Brady's laugh was immediate. "Yeah, right. He really doesn't know you very well."

Erin grinned. "Why, thank you. I think that's the nicest compliment I've received today."

"I assume you, ah, corrected his erroneous assumption?"

"I did manage to drive that point home, yes. Rather emphatically."

Brady chuckled. "I can imagine."

She nodded in appreciation of his support. *See, being a friend wasn't so hard.* He could do this.

She went on. "As soon as I got in the office, I tried to get Henley to arrange some time one-on-one to go over my ideas, away from Todd's endless interruptions, but it didn't happen. Todd intervened, and Henley made it obvious he was going to go with Todd's advice over mine, even perhaps over his own instincts. That's when I realized it was time to cut bait and fish in other waters. I'm not much for catching sharks."

"Fishing metaphors? Don't tell me you like to throw

out a line, too? Between that and your personal home-theater system over there, I might have to rethink my entire position on marriage."

"You teased me with that once before, I believe," she said with a laugh. "But to set the record straight, no, I don't fish." She shuddered. "Too scaly. And they eat worms. Gross."

"Ah, so there's a girly-girl lurking beneath that tomboy exterior somewhere."

Now she looked shocked. "You think my exterior is tomboyish?" She laughed. "And just moments ago you seemed perfectly aware of my feminine allure."

"You are a multifaceted woman, Ms. Mahoney," he responded, amused. "I'll safely leave it at that."

She grinned. "Smart man. And I like that. Multifaceted. Who said all cops were crude and uncouth?"

She reached for her glass but bumped it instead, wobbling it dangerously close to the edge. Brady lunged for it just as she did and they both slipped off the couch onto their knees...and watched the glass hit the carpet, soaking a circle of it with wine.

"Dammit!" She reached for the glass at the same time he did.

"I've got the glass," he said. "Got anything to mop this up with?"

They both looked from the spill to each other and simultaneously realized just how close their faces were to one another.

He managed to put the glass on the coffee table without taking his eyes off hers.

The silence deepened as neither of them moved.

"Brady, I—"

"Do you have any idea how green your eyes look in this room?" he asked in a hushed voice. He'd no intention of speaking, the words had just tumbled from his brain directly to his tongue, his mind too muddled to stop them.

"Uh. No," she said, her own voice a bit husky as well. "I didn't."

He very slowly lifted his hand and brushed a few loose tendrils off her face. "Spicy."

"What?" she asked a bit breathlessly.

"Your scent. It's very…dark." He let his finger run down the side of her face. "And erotic."

Her pupils shot wide and her throat worked. "It's, um— Thanks."

"It suits you. Part of you anyway."

"Part of me?"

He lifted his other hand to her hair, willing himself not to think about the fact that he'd promised himself this was precisely what he wasn't going to do here.

"Yeah," he said gruffly. "Part of you is spicy and erotic." He toyed with her hair. He wrapped the curl around his finger and rubbed it along her cheekbone. At her audible gasp, he smiled. "And part of you is private, soft."

She opened her mouth and he was certain she was going to object. He didn't want to let her. He didn't want her to rationalize or debate what was happening. In fact, he didn't want her to do any thinking at all. So he stopped her the best way he knew how. He kissed her.

11

ERIN KNEW she should shift away, turn her head. She'd read the intent in his eyes the moment they'd both lost track of the wine. And yet she remained anchored to the spot, heedless of the fact that the spot was growing increasingly damp.

His eyes were dark with want. And what he wanted was her. The hell with the wine-soaked carpet. Hadn't this been exactly where she'd hoped this was headed?

His lips touched hers. Warm, confident, demanding. He cupped her face and turned her head so he could take the kiss deeper. Her body responded like a live wire, and she realized instantly that this would not be a simple releasing of tension.

This was... Dear God, she had no idea what this was, only that she wanted it more than she wanted her next breath.

"Erin."

His voice was even deeper, rougher. He pushed his tongue into her mouth, dueled with hers, taunted her into responding. And respond she did. He continued to push her, yet pull her in more deeply.

She grew achingly aware that her bed was mere steps away. She could have more of this. More of him. More of...everything.

His hands moved down her arms and he shifted his lips from her mouth to work his magic along her jaw and down to the tender spot on her neck, just below her ear. And now that her mouth was free, there was nothing to muffle the moans that pushed up from somewhere deep inside her.

He settled his wide hands on her hips and tugged her forward. As soon as her hips bumped between his, she felt just how much he wanted her. Very badly. Her inner thighs tightened against the instant ache that sweet pressure created. The need to take, demand, have, filled her so swiftly she couldn't think clearly.

This was out of control. She should be worrying about that, thinking about the ramifications, deciding if she should pursue or retreat. But right at that moment she was about two seconds and a slight shift of the hard bulge pressing insistently between her legs away from climaxing. Her body overruled any danger signals her brain sent out.

"Brady." It was a rough plea, a demand.

And then that tantalizing pressure was gone and he was pulling her up. Her head swam, she was so dizzy with need. "What—"

"I'm not doing this in a puddle of white wine." His voice was strained, rough.

"But—"

He tugged her to him as they both struggled to stand. She opened her mouth to— She had no idea. Thankfully, she was spared figuring it out when that incredible pressure found its way to the juncture of her legs once again.

"Hold on," he commanded.

"Thank God."

He lifted her up. "Wrap your legs around me." He was already shifting them there even as he made his way toward her bedroom.

She locked her heels behind him, then groaned. Loudly. That one extra inch of snugness put her right on the edge. "Brady. Brady, please." She clamped her heels more tightly and started to tremble she was so close. "I just need—"

"I know, I know." He staggered into her room and they both tumbled across her bed. Hands moved in a tangle as they fought with their clothes. Both of them were swearing by the time they managed to yank everything off. They all but dived back at each other. Somewhere in her mind she thought about slowing down so she could run her hands over him, look at him, enjoy him. Later, she promised herself. Much later.

Brady pulled her under him, his dark eyes wild with want. Erin thrilled at the sight. Maybe she'd known it would be like this with him, primal, insistent, demanding. Maybe that was what had made her bold enough to present him with her plan in the first place. He would give and he would take and there would be nothing left over when they were done. Wasn't that what release was all about?

He shifted between her legs and she was already arching off the bed to reach him. He brushed against her and she bit back a scream as her muscles clenched painfully tight. "I'm—so—close," she ground out.

"Yeah." He was panting. "I know. Jesus, do I know." Then his expression went painfully tight.

Somewhere in her fevered brain she registered this was not a good sign, but it was really hard to tell her body to stop all its arching and seeking. "What?" she demanded breathlessly. "Dammit, what's wrong?"

He laughed harshly. "Always...bossy."

She wanted to laugh. Next time they'd laugh. And be playful and take their time. Dear God, she might not survive to the next time if he didn't Do Something Right Now.

"Protection," he managed to say, sweat beading his forehead.

His expression was so fierce, so...perfect, it took her a moment to realize what he was saying. "Oh. It's okay."

"Sure?"

Her hips bumped up again. He brushed against her again. She almost whimpered. So close. "Trust me," she forced out.

He grinned then, his chest heaving. "Now I know I'm crazy." And then he grabbed her hips and with a guttural groan of pleasure that made Erin's entire body vibrate, he pushed all the way inside her with one deep, gliding thrust.

And she came. Instantly and ferociously.

She wasn't even done peaking before she realized that once was not going to be enough. A moment after that, she realized this was not going to be a concern. Brady was more than up to the task. Beautifully so, perfectly so.

He moved inside her so completely, so fully, she gasped in amazement as one wave crested, peaked, then another one built right behind it. Had she known there was anything like this in existence, she'd have dedicated her life to finding it. And keeping it selfishly all to herself for all eternity.

Somehow she didn't think Brady was going to go for that plan. Brady. She was really feeling this, doing this, wanting more of this...with Brady. She forced her eyes to open and looked up at him, expecting to find his eyes shut as he guided his wonderful body repeatedly and perfectly into hers.

What she found instead rocked her. His gaze was locked intently, almost fiercely on her. And it wasn't a mindless, lost-in-the-passion gaze either. It was alert, aware and looking damn possessive. Another climax ripped through her, having little to do with his body inside hers...and everything to do with how his gaze reached inside her.

"Brady," she rasped, stunned.

He said nothing, but remained focused on her as he pushed into her again...and again. Dragging her up to that edge one more time, his gaze telling her with every stroke that he knew his command over her in that moment was absolute and he was reveling in that power.

But there was something else there, too. A wild, almost desperate edge that all but begged her to do something, anything, to end this, or balance it, explain it. But she didn't want to...and therein lay her own power. And she reveled in it just as much. Right now,

right here, her command over him was just as powerful and just as equal as his over her. That realization
brought with it a little panic, which she shoved aside.

Her body moved with his naturally, joyfully. Their
eyes remained locked on one another, making this connection deeper, more intimate. She realized she could
drown in this, willingly let herself sink beneath the surface of it and never want to come up for air again. Panic
crept in again as the risk grew. "Brady, I—"

He shook his head, cutting her off by capturing her
lips beneath his, plunging his tongue between them
and taking her mouth in the same insistent fashion he
was taking her body. Despite whatever panic they felt,
he continued to demand from her the same joyful, endless response she'd given him in every other way.

She tried not to think about the way he'd just looked
at her, into her, so deeply...far more deeply than his
body had penetrated hers. As his kisses continued, she
let her eyes drift shut and allowed the sensation of feeling him all over her, inside her, everywhere she
wanted him, to wash through her until she finally gave
herself completely to it.

The final release, when it came, was so powerful, it
blanked everything from her mind except that exact
moment when they'd both rocketed over the final
edge. The sensations of his own shattering climax vibrated throughout her entire being. His mouth never
left hers. She had felt his groan when release finally
overtook him, tasted it, consumed it.

And then there was nothing left but the trembling.
He shifted off her, and when she reached for him, not

wanting him to leave her just yet, he curled one of her hands in his...but left her all the same.

He rolled onto his back beside her and she could hear them both breathing heavily. She wanted to say something to him. Tell him how unbelievable she felt. But she couldn't make herself break the silence. She willed him to silence, too, afraid that when they finally spoke, this...whatever it had been...would change, mutate into something other than what she knew it had been.

A release valve, huh? She wanted to laugh. She wanted to cry. Well, she'd found that all right. And so much more. Dear God, she'd discovered the true meaning of more. Almost more than she could handle. Almost.

Her eyes closed and she fell back to that electrifying moment when she'd opened her eyes to find him looking at her like that. *Like that. Like what, Erin? What was that look?*

She wasn't sure. But she did know it was exclusive and it was theirs. Only they would share it. Never had she felt that sort of connection with anyone. Soul deep, more unifying than their joined bodies, but made more special because of their joined bodies.

Did she want to know what it meant to him? Did she dare? He was a man who didn't make commitments. She knew damn well no matter how he felt about what had just happened wouldn't change that fact one iota. She'd always known that. Hell, she'd been the one to lay down the stupid rules in the first place. Hadn't that been why she thought he'd be so perfect for this? Oh, he was perfect all right.

Who was the joke on now?

So now what in the hell did she do? She'd sworn this would just be physical. She also knew there was no way that was possible now. She wasn't romanticizing, dammit, she wasn't. But that look... She'd never forget that moment. Ever. No matter what he said, or tried to explain. She realized she'd never be able to ask him about it for that reason. He'd try to explain it away. And she'd hate him for that.

Okay. Maybe she was romanticizing a little. She squeezed her eyes shut. He'd laugh himself sick if he knew the silly romantic thoughts that were running through her mind right now. So she wouldn't tell him.

Which meant this would be it. She couldn't do this again. She'd surely end up humiliating herself by saying something she shouldn't, asking for something he couldn't or wouldn't give. So much for her bold proclamation that she could handle a jump-n-run. *Yeah, thanks, Gina.*

But he was still here. Their first and only time wasn't over yet. And if she was only going to have him for one night, then she was damn well going to do her best to make it last all night.

She opened her eyes and slowly turned her head toward his. Had he been staring at her the way he had before, she had no idea what she'd have done. Probably run to the bathroom and locked herself in. Or thrown herself at him, gushing all sorts of embarrassing confessions.

But he wasn't. She told herself she was relieved.

His eyes were closed, his chest moving up and down as his breathing slowly smoothed out. *Just for one night, Erin.* She could handle one night. Couldn't she?

BRADY JUMPED when he felt her warm hand slowly skim across his thigh. He wanted to groan. In pleasure or exhaustion he wasn't sure. So he bit back his reaction.

He had no idea what had just happened between them, but he was pretty damn sure it was no release-valve thing like she'd explained. Or maybe it had been for her. And damn if she hadn't released. Over and over.

Sweet Jesus, he'd never have done this if he'd had any idea how completely intoxicating she'd be. All of her. Her body, her mind, the way she looked at him, responded to him, took him, gave to him. He willed himself to resist the siren call of those long fingers now slowly moving up his chest. No way could he want her, want anything remotely physical, at this moment. He was wasted, satiated, totaled. Sleep should be overtaking him any second.

Get up, Brady. Right now. He needed to move while he still could, and gather his clothes, say God knows what to her...and get the hell out of here.

Except he couldn't ignore the way her fingers slowly rubbed over his chest. Damn but he'd had no idea a man's nipples could be so sensitive. Not his anyway. What was she doing to him? He really had to make her stop. And he would. In just a moment.

"Erin—" He just needed her to stop for one second, so he could gather his strength and get up.

"Shh. I want to touch you. I didn't get the chance before." He heard the smile in her voice. "We were sort of in a hurry."

"Yeah." *Scintillating, O'Keefe. You're a real conversationalist.* But it was all he could manage. He'd just managed to slow his heart down to the point that it would stay safely inside his chest…and she was busily jacking it up again. Amongst other things. The woman had bewitched him. There was no other explanation for the way his body was responding. *Traitor,* he told himself.

Only he wasn't buying that either. If it had only been about the sex, he'd already be standing and getting dressed, stumbling through that awkward goodbye moment and getting the hell out. Only this wasn't feeling all that awkward. In fact, it was feeling good. Damn good.

All he had to do was lie here and let her keep touching him. No real reason to stop her, he told himself. After all, she'd made the rules. She told him he could trust her. And he had. Erin wouldn't jeopardize herself, so he felt pretty safe there. So, this was okay. He could just stay here a little longer and nothing that hadn't already been changed would really change any further.

Right?

She traced her fingers slowly over his face, through his hair, down around the rim of his ears, along his collarbone, then skated them over his chest again. He shivered with pleasure…and a little trepidation. It made no sense, but he realized he was suddenly feeling the tiniest bit exposed to her. Which was totally ridiculous considering what they'd just been doing. It was her eyes, he thought. Even with his own closed now, he could feel them on him like a caress. And he thought of that moment, when she'd opened her eyes while she was beneath him, and he was buried so deeply inside her sweet body. She'd looked at him, into him, in that way only she ever had. Or maybe ever would.

He jerked his eyes open then and his hand came up to still hers. His instincts screamed at him to move, to leave. He couldn't shake that moment out of his mind and he knew right then that everything had indeed changed. He braced himself, for what he honestly couldn't say, and turned his head to look at her, his fingers still tightly covering hers.

She was looking at him. But this was different. Her mouth was curved in that smile she had, the look in her eyes was knowing. Hungry. He'd have wondered at the very probability of that if his own body hadn't leaped in instant recognition of that hunger. He let out a relieved sigh. So maybe things hadn't changed after all. He'd just been hormonally overwhelmed earlier. Maybe there was no risk here, except that she might kill him before the night was over. He thought about that, then decided what the hell, blocked everything else out and pulled her on top of him.

He swallowed her delighted moan and didn't take his mouth off her until she made that whimpering sound that drove him crazy. He rolled her beneath him, looking down at her as he pinned her hands to the bed. She merely lifted one eyebrow at him, supremely confident that while she might be pinned beneath him, she firmly held the upper hand.

"Last time was a little...rough," he said.

Her mouth curved into a slow smile. "I've heard that about cops."

"With you being so multi...faceted and all, I figure you might be able to show me how to slow things down. Do this all refined and polite-like."

She almost spluttered into laughter, but controlled it. "Refined, huh?" She glanced upward at his hands pinning hers down. "You'll have to release me. If you aren't afraid of my multi...facetedness, that is."

He instantly lifted his hands, even went so far as to lift off of her and sit back on his heels. "Just tell me what to do. And how to do it."

"So cooperative. I'm impressed." She slid her legs up beneath her and kneeled on the bed in front of him. "First, we refined individuals usually prefer to clean up...you know, afterward."

"Do you prefer to do this cleaning up alone?"

"Oh no, never." She slid off the bed and held out her hand. "Lather my...back?"

He grinned. She was more fun than he'd ever had. "Sure. But only if you'll lather...mine." He took her hand, but somehow they never made it past the door frame. He had to taste her, couldn't wait a single second longer, in fact.

Maybe it was the way she laughed with him, so easily, or the way she dared him with that look of hers.

Any other reasons—like that look that had thrown him for a loop earlier—those were too dangerous to contemplate. So he didn't. Keep it simple, keep it fun.

But damn he had to taste her right now or he'd die. He stopped in the bathroom doorway and pulled her to him as he leaned back on the jamb. He found her mouth so easily, so perfectly ready for him, he groaned at the rightness of it. Then she was leaning into him, demanding and taking equally. That turned him on even further.

He liked it that she didn't wait, that she took what she wanted, demanded it. And that she also gave so generously. No lying back and letting him call the shots, for her pleasure or his. It was incredibly arousing knowing he had pleased her so completely...and he knew he had. Did she realize how unique this entire time had been to him? Had this been as unique to her?

Shut up and kiss her, O'Keefe. Enjoy the moment, enjoy tonight. Don't ruin it by worrying about every little thing. He had the feeling he'd be doing plenty of that later, anyway.

She pulled him into the bathroom, their lips still joined. She reached in and tugged the shower on, but kept her mouth firmly on his. He took and let her take as the room filled with steam. Their kiss went on...and on. It should have been jacking them up to that frantic fever pitch they'd been at earlier. But somehow the kiss slowed, deepened...defined.

He charted her face with his fingertips as he tasted her softly, gently. Then he wove his fingers into her hair, and kissed her like something to be cherished.

It was then Brady really began to worry.

12

ERIN DIDN'T GET as far as the shower before reality came crashing back. Well, beeping back. In the form of Brady's pager.

With the shower pounding next to them, it had taken a moment for the sound to penetrate the fog. Actually, Erin never would have heard it, but Brady had spent enough years with lives depending on his hearing that beeping noise that he picked up the sound almost immediately. He'd sworn loudly, as had she when he ducked out the door to snatch up the pager. But he hadn't promised he'd only be a moment and then they'd resume where they'd left off. She supposed she was at least thankful for that. No promises that couldn't be kept.

He'd come back in, with his cop face...and his trousers on. She'd quickly grabbed her robe off the back of the door, feeling somehow exposed now that reality had intruded on their private little world. She'd nodded in complete understanding when he'd explained he'd had no choice, that he had to go. After all, she was an adult and it wasn't as if she hadn't known going in that something like this might happen. Wasn't this why she'd told Gina she'd never get serious about Brady?

As he dressed, she'd rested against the doorjamb between the bathroom and bedroom, telling herself it was better this way. No awkward morning goodbyes, or even late-evening ones. It would end as abruptly as it had begun. No need to explain or say anything. He seemed to understand that as he silently dressed. He tugged on his holster, which underscored her resolve that this was for the best. He followed that with his jacket, eliciting a small smile from her. Not surprisingly, it didn't look any more rumpled than usual. Unlike herself.

She caught her reflection in the mirror over her dresser. Tousled was probably the word for how she looked. Tousled and well pleasured. Like a cat who'd lain in the sun all day after spending the morning lapping rich, thick cream.

She pulled her gaze back to him as he paused at the door and looked back to her. She made herself smile. It was that or fling herself at him and beg him to come back when whatever had called him away no longer needed his attention. *She* needed his attention. Craved it. "Goodbye, Brady," she said softly, hearing the finality in the words. He must have, too.

But he held her gaze for such a long moment, she felt her resolve waver. Okay, it more than wavered. It was bordering on crumbling to dust when he finally nodded and replied with a gruff, "Yeah."

Then he was gone.

She stayed right where she was, hoping the doorjamb would keep her upright until she heard the front door close. Then she could slide into a boneless heap and start the long agonizing process of analyzing every last detail of this wondrous evening. And figuring out how she was going to get past it.

She strained to hear the click of the front door, her knees already trembling. What she heard instead was a sharply emitted epithet, then his heavy tread coming back across her living-room carpet. He burst into the room looking larger than life, and so damn good she had to lock her knees against the urge to run to him. He'd probably just forgotten something.

As it turned out, he had. Her.

He never slowed, crossing the room with his gaze squarely on her, that intent, possessive look all over his face. She froze in place, not daring to believe that look again. Still unsure what it had meant that first time. But she did nothing to avoid him as he tugged her hard into his arms and kissed her so thoroughly she was too breathless to speak when he finally let her go.

He looked into her eyes for a long moment, then suddenly said, "It will probably be late by the time I'm done," as if the words had been torn from him. His gaze continued to search hers.

She nodded. It was all she could do. What was he saying? Asking?

"Probably too late to…to come back here."

She didn't nod this time. The words simply tumbled out of her. "I don't care." She probably should, for lots of reasons. But the truth was she didn't. Not if it meant this wasn't over yet. She'd care later. Hopefully much later.

His eyes glowed at her response. "Yeah," he said

roughly. Then a grin teased the corners of his mouth, as if he couldn't quite believe he was this lucky. "Okay." He kissed her again, grinning fully when he lifted his mouth from hers. "Good."

Erin touched her lips, wondering just what she'd done as she watched him walk away once again. This time she didn't even make it till he was halfway across the living room before sliding to the floor.

DON'T THINK ABOUT IT, Brady. *The job is waiting. Think about the job.* The fact that he even had to remind himself was the biggest warning signal he could have asked for. If he'd been even close to being in his right mind, he'd have listened to it. Probably. He couldn't worry about it now. He had a dead body to deal with.

But even as he called in his location and estimated time of arrival, cutting across the dark city streets toward the crime scene, his thoughts remained on Erin. On her actually wanting him to come back. And damn but he did want to go back. He'd honestly tried to leave, knowing from her silence as he dressed that she was tacitly agreeing to simply let this be a one-night thing, no explanations, no apologies. No regrets. What more could a guy ask for?

He'd almost been there, almost to the door. But it had just felt…unfinished. He'd told himself he needed one last kiss, something to finalize it. He'd kiss her, smile, get that dry smile of hers in return so he'd know she was really okay with everything, then leave.

But that plan had gone all to hell the moment he'd walked back into her bedroom and seen the naked hunger leap into her eyes. A hunger he'd matched, mind, body and soul. He'd never, not ever, been a possessive man. Had, in fact, gone out of his way to make sure any woman he was involved with knew for certain he never would be. He'd stayed true to that, with no doubts, his entire adult life. Until that moment.

It defined what had passed between them when he'd been inside her, that hunger he saw. The same hunger he felt, the kind a starving man would feel. It explained to him, in no uncertain terms, that he was well and truly in a deep load of trouble here. Because he absolutely felt possessive now. He'd wanted to lay claim, right then and there. And he'd been greedy, too. Because he'd wanted it all. Heart, body, soul, mind. All his.

He took a corner and lowered the window, hoping cool air would clear his head. Probably going back to her place later would be the antidote for this...whatever it was he was feeling. Surely he'd go back and realize it had all been some kind of hormonally induced lunacy. He'd see her again and wonder what the hell had possessed him to think there was something else going on here besides two people who just happened to have a spectacular way of making the earth move. Yeah, that was it. Probably.

Then it would be over. Just this one night, then they'd move on. Enjoy the memory of it. He wouldn't think of her and wonder what if, because he'd realize when he went back that he didn't want the responsibility of her feelings, her needs, her desires. And he sure as hell didn't want her to be responsible for his. No way. His life, his needs, his desires were his to fulfill. First, last and always.

He couldn't want Erin in that equation. It would lead to certain disaster. A disaster he'd seen play out so many times before. So he'd take what they'd shared tonight and be thankful he'd figured out that he didn't need more than that. More always spelled trouble.

He fingered his cell phone as he drove, then realized he was unconsciously punching in her home number. He hadn't even realized he'd committed it to memory. He put the phone down, then picked it right back up again. Maybe he should call and cancel, let it be over now. He swore under his breath even as he laughed at himself. God, he'd never been this messed up over a woman. He punched in the number, knowing this was the right thing to do.

"Hello?"

Brady's heart sped up. Just like that. One word from her and he was primed and ready to go. Yep, ending it now was smart, prudent. He should be damn proud of himself for being on top of this. "Yeah, hello. It's me."

There was a pause and he smiled despite himself as he pictured that wry curve of those unbelievable lips of hers.

"Me, huh?" she said. "I don't think I know any Me."

"Oh, you know this me. Very well, I believe." Jesus, he was flirting. How in the hell did she do that? He was calling to end this. *So end it already, O'Keefe. What are you waiting for?*

"Oh," she said, amusement clear in her tone. *"That me."*

Another pause and in the space of those few, torturous seconds he was hard as a rock. This was insane.

"Why yes," she went on, "I do believe I recall now. Some vague notion of a shower I ended up taking alone. Was that you who was supposed to lather my...back?"

"Yeah," he choked out, unable to keep from visualizing that scene in his mind. "That would be me."

Then her voice abruptly changed. "Uh-oh. Did something happen, Brady?" She was all business now.

The sudden change threw him. "What?"

"I just realized that maybe you were calling to tell me you wouldn't be able to come back."

I am. Only the words weren't coming out of his mouth.

"I'm really sorry," she went on. "But I...I understand. Really."

Take the easy out. One word and it will all be over, no harm done. "No. At least, I don't know if I can or not. I'm not on the scene yet." Dammit, what was he doing?

"So why are you calling me?"

Damn good question, O'Keefe. Surprisingly, he began to laugh. "I have no idea," he said, as honest as he'd ever been in his life.

There was a pause, then a little surprised laughter from her end. "Okay."

"I'm not sure of that either," he murmured, wondering how he'd let things get so out of hand. He pulled up to the scene at that moment, red lights were flashing, police cruisers lined the street and people clustered and clung to each other. Finally some semblance of sanity returned. This was chaos he understood. "I'm here. I'll call you when I know what's going on."

She'd obviously heard the shift in his tone. Hers shifted as well. "Just do what you need to do, Brady. I'll be here if you get done in time. Okay?"

He threw the car into park, but just sat there.

"Brady?"

"Yeah. Yeah, okay." He blew out a deep breath, knowing that rather than end it, he had somehow taken another step. One he wasn't sure he was fully prepared to take. But he took it anyway. "I'll call you, Erin." Then he disconnected and climbed out of his car. He walked away from the confusion he'd just landed himself in, moving almost gratefully toward something he knew a whole lot more about. Homicide.

As he neared the buzzing crowd, he was already shifting to the task at hand. Yet a small part of him wondered if maybe, just maybe, there should be more to life than this. If maybe, just maybe, it would be nice to occasionally set this insanity aside, even for a few hours.

Especially if those few hours were spent like his last few had.

But the key word in all that was *occasionally*. Because, like it or not, his job was a demanding mistress and her demands could be untimely and sometimes downright cruel. And who wanted to settle for being his occasional companion? Certainly not Erin. She wanted white picket fences, dogs and kids. He felt an odd ache when he pictured that scenario, her standing in the middle of it, smiling as she waited for him in the midst

of domestic chaos. It amazed him that it had appealed
to him, even for a brief moment. But when he tried to
put himself in that scene, what he saw were flashes of
the increasingly unhappy family life he'd been raised
in.

And that was one path he wasn't going to go down.
Especially not with Erin. She deserved far better.

His debate ended in the next instant as a young offi-
cer stepped forward to tell him the identity of the vic-
tim.

ERIN TOLD HERSELF she was absolutely not waiting up
for him. She certainly wasn't staying up because she
was caught in the supposed riveting suspense in the
mystery she'd been looking at and not reading for the
last thirty minutes. She slapped it down on the coffee
table and grabbed the remote. She let the soothing
sounds of sports highlights fill the room as she got up
to refresh her coffee.

"You're waiting up for him," she muttered. "Face
it."

Okay, so maybe she was. Or maybe she was simply
dying to find out who won the PBA Canton, Ohio,
Bowling Open. And who knew that high-school cheer-
leaders could throw people that high in the air? She sat
back on the couch and flicked through several other
sports channels, then shut the television off and
flipped the remote in the same direction as the aban-
doned paperback. Okay, so she was definitely waiting
up for him. She stared at the phone. "So call me, dammit."

It was now past two in the morning. She and Gina had a meeting at ten to go over any ramifications or potential fallout from ending their business with the mayor. It would be in the papers in the morning. Probably had made the eleven o'clock news as a mention in the ongoing campaign coverage. But she'd been doing other things at eleven o'clock.

She let her head drop back on the edge of the couch and stared at the ceiling. Lord, had she been doing something. Despite the late hour her body responded very clearly to the mental stimuli of her visualizing just what she'd been doing. And with whom.

She sat up. So, did that mean she just wanted him back for more spectacular sex? She laughed. Hell yes. She wasn't stupid. She sighed and let her head drop back again. But there was no getting around the rest of it. And there was most certainly a rest of it. In fact, Brady was a whole lot more than she'd bargained for. He was direct, honest and straightforward—in bed and out. There was no game playing with him, but he had a sense of humor and didn't take himself, or anything else, all that seriously. Probably the only way he dealt with the side of life he was exposed to on a daily basis.

She wondered what he was doing right now. Being that he was a homicide detective, she had a fairly good idea it wasn't pretty. What did he do after a night like this? Dead bodies and crime scenes, possibly hysterical or devastated people involved. At some point the night would come to an end, then what? Her lips quirked. Probably back to his desk, rumpled suit and all, to write up endless reports. Her expression sobered. But after that? Did he go home and sleep, only to get up and go back again? He didn't talk much about his life outside the job. Probably because he didn't have one. Which meant what?

She groaned. "Which means you've gone and fallen for the worst man you could have fallen for."

The phone rang just then, making her start badly. Her heart continued to race as she reached for it, but in anticipation now. "Hello?"

"It's me."

She would have smiled, maybe teased him again, but he sounded unbearably weary. "Hi, Me. You don't sound so hot."

"Yeah." He paused, then blew out a breath. "I know it's late and I'm sorry to wake you, but I didn't want you to worry or wonder... Hell, I just looked at my watch. I didn't realize it was this late. You were probably sleeping. I'm sorry."

Erin debated for about three seconds on whether to tell him, but honesty had gotten them this far. "No. I couldn't sleep. I was waiting to hear from you. I tried watching some national high-school cheerleading competition thing. Too damn perky for two in the morning, though. I had to shut them off."

He chuckled and she thought she'd never heard anything sweeter than that. His life might be one long stretch of shift work, but she could at least do this. It didn't feel like much, but— Well, no, that was a lie. It felt good to be the one he called, the one who might lift his spirits after a hard night, even if only for a moment.

Jesus, she'd really gone around the bend, hadn't she?

"I have news for you," he said, breaking into her reverie. "The homicide tonight. It's likely it was connected to the Sanderson case. I wanted to be the one to tell you. It was Bradford Pitts."

Erin froze, her throat closed over. The reporter Bradford Pitts? He'd been sort of sleazy and all, but she'd never imagined— "Why? Do you know who did it?"

"Apparently he's been snooping around in the Han family business, still working the angle with Sanderson. I guess he got too close to finding the answer."

"But he's not much more than a tabloid reporter. What could he have known that was so threatening?"

"That's what we have to find out."

Erin slumped back on the couch. "Okay," she said quietly, still stunned by this turn of events. "I'm glad you called and told me. Thank you."

"Yeah," he said gruffly. There was a pause, then, "Listen, Erin, I—"

"Don't worry about it," she broke in, knowing what he was going to say. "I understand. You're going to be tied up for a long time on this, I'm sure." She paused, knowing he was a long way from getting some sleep. It was one thing staying up all night working on some press release or ad campaign; Brady was staying up in order to track down a killer. "I don't know how you do it."

He gave a short, humorless laugh. "I'm beginning to wonder about that myself."

She smiled now, but it was a melancholy one. So this

was it, she thought. Probably better this way. God, she hated that. "Well, we're all thankful you do it."

"Someone's got to."

Yeah, she thought. Someone who can't imagine doing anything else. "They have the right man for the job then. Good night, Brady. I hope you get some sleep soon. Even superheroes need to take a break sometime."

He didn't laugh as she'd hoped he would. He didn't say anything, in fact. So much for being the one he could turn to, the one who knew the right thing to say.

The silence spun out, stopped being awkward and started being...something else. She felt the tension spike, and her grip on the phone tightened. *Say it,* she silently urged. *Just one word to let me know this isn't over.* God, how pathetic was she? But she couldn't stop hoping anyway.

Finally he blew out a long, deep breath. "Right," he said. Then, more quietly, more resigned, "Right."

"Brady?" *Shut up, Erin, just let the poor man go.* But she couldn't. Foolish or not, pathetic or not, she couldn't just let him walk away. And then she was blurting out the words herself. "If you need somewhere to go and take that superhero cape off for a while..." *Oh God.* She took a steadying breath. It didn't help. "You can come here," she finished in a rush. She squeezed her eyes shut. "Okay?"

"You're really something else, Erin Mahoney."

"Something else good?" she asked, her heart pounding so hard it was tough to get that wry note just right. "Or something else bad?"

He chuckled then and she could picture him raking his fingers through his hair. "I guess we're going to find out, aren't we?"

Yes! Erin pumped her fist and did a little dance with her feet. When she thought she could speak without sounding like a giddy schoolgirl who had just been asked to the senior prom, she said, "I guess we are."

She had just taken a very big step off a potentially very high cliff. But at the moment, she felt as if she could fly. And that was all that mattered for now.

13

HE SHOULD GO HOME. Take a shower, catch as much uninterrupted sleep as possible. God knew he was dead on his feet. He couldn't even feel his feet. And one more cup of that god-awful coffee, his stomach lining would go numb as well. But somehow, instead of heading crosstown to his generically furnished little apartment, he ended up pulling into a guest space beneath Erin's building.

"Go home, Brady." He laid his weary head on the steering wheel. If Erin had half a brain in her head, she'd tell him the same thing. He pried open one eye and looked at the dashboard clock. Seven o'clock—p.m. He hadn't slept in... He didn't want to do the math. All he knew was that the last place he'd been relaxed was approximately twelve floors above his head. And, like a homing pigeon, that was where his body wanted to return to.

He wasn't even sure if she was home. He'd called her once in the middle of the day, but had gotten Gina instead. She'd told him Erin had several meetings with prospective clients that afternoon, then was planning on calling it a day. With no small amount of amusement, Gina had pointed out that her business partner hadn't had much sleep and seemed a little off-kilter today. Then she'd sobered and asked about the investigation, which he'd not been at liberty to discuss.

So why he felt the need to talk it over with Erin he had no idea. Maybe it was because she brought a sort of levelheaded, yet no-holds-barred type of common sense to the table. He wanted to bounce ideas off of her, get her input.

"Yeah, right. You just want to get her in bed, O'Keefe." He swore under his breath and slammed out of the car, half hoping she wouldn't be home so he'd have no choice but to return to his own. Because his reasons for being here had almost nothing to do with sex.

Five minutes later she was answering the door and he forgot every reason he'd come up with for being anywhere but right where he stood.

She immediately moved toward him and ran a hand over his lapel. "Man, and here I thought this suit couldn't get any more wrinkled."

He managed to smile at that. "Hello to you, too." He resisted the urge to smooth his hair, straighten that lapel. Like it would have done any good anyway. Except it would have made her laugh. God he loved to hear her laugh. "Sorry I didn't call first."

"I'm not. I love surprises." Then she grabbed him by both lapels, pulled him inside her apartment and kicked the door shut behind him. Her lips were hard on his before he knew what was happening.

But it didn't take him long to figure it out. He was tired, but he'd have to be dead not to respond to her.

He wasn't dead as it turned out. But when he went to reach for her, she shook her head.

"That was just a hello kiss. Now you're going to straight to my bathroom and taking a good-night shower." She didn't wait for an argument, although he wasn't trying real hard to find one. Okay, not at all. Getting naked and soapy sounded like just fine to him. So he let her shuffle him to her bathroom.

"I seem to recall another time and place in this very room," he said, then stumbled as she started peeling off his clothes. He could really get used to this.

"Yes, well, I don't think I'll be joining you this time, Supercop."

He pouted. Actually pouted. But it seemed like the only rational response. "But you promised to lather my back."

"That was yesterday, this is today." She reached in the shower and yanked the faucet on. Then she reached for his buckle.

He called a halt to things right there. "If you're not providing any tub toys for me, I'm not sharing my toys with you either."

"Oh. Well. I hate it when a grown man won't share his, um, toys."

He shrugged. "Then maybe we should renegotiate this."

She walked to the door. "Shampoo is on the shelf under the spray. Soap on the shelf in the back. I'll be out here when you're done."

"Spoilsport."

"Me? Never. Come find me when you're done.

There's plenty of hot water, so take your time and enjoy." He started to argue, but she raised her finger. "Lose gracefully, Brady. It will earn you brownie points for later."

"I love brownies."

She was smiling as the door shut between them.

He finished stripping and climbed under the shower. Any protestations he'd had about her plan died the instant the hot water began beating on his back. He automatically reached up to shift the showerhead to massage mode, then realized she didn't have that feature. *I'll have to fix that,* he thought. Then froze in the act of reaching for the soap. Where the hell had that come from? One romp in bed and a shower and he was redesigning her living space to accommodate him?

He should be concerned. Very concerned. But, the truth was, he was beat, the water felt good and all he wanted to do was wash the last eighteen hours of work off himself so he could go find Erin. *And what, O'Keefe?* He hummed under his breath as the suds ran off his body and down the drain. Right at that moment, he honestly didn't care. As long as she was with him while they did it.

As IT TURNED OUT, what they did was sleep. Or he did anyway. Helluva way to impress a lady, he thought, eyes drooping shut as she rubbed his back. He was stretched out facedown across her bed, which is where she'd basically pushed him when he'd stumbled out of the shower wrapped in nothing more than a towel. His clothes had disappeared.

He'd had every intention of rolling right back over and pulling her down on top of him, but then she was straddling his back and doing something that felt pretty close to nirvana along his spine. After which she'd moved to his shoulders and he'd given up the fight.

"Next time it will be your turn," he said groggily.

"Damn straight it will be," she'd returned. "And don't think you can come crawling here after playing superhero and expect this kind of treatment every time."

"Won't," he mumbled, fighting the long, deep slide into sleep.

"What time do you have to be out of here?"

"Hmm?" God, her hands were pure magic. He never wanted her to stop touching him.

"Never mind. I'll make sure you get up in time to go home and change. Does 5:00 a.m. sound about right to you?"

"Five. Meeting. Six."

He thought he heard her chuckle. Or maybe he was already dreaming. Maybe he was home right now and this was all a dream. He smiled sleepily. Best damn dream he could recall ever having.

ERIN LEANED DOWN and kissed the back of Brady's neck. He was down for the count. She crawled off him and thought about trying to turn him around so his head was on the pillows, but one tug on his arm and leg convinced her she'd never manage it. Given the somewhat adorable smile on his face, he didn't seem to be suffering for having his legs half hanging off the bed. Her bed. Of which there was now no room for her to be in. Unless she wanted to lie sprawled sideways the way he was.

She laughed and shook her head. "Sure planned that one out well, didn't I?" She tucked a pillow under his head, put his pager in his hand, then snagged another pillow and a throw blanket for herself. She paused in the doorway after flicking off the lights. The glow from the living-room lamp played across the bed, highlighting his big sprawling body. Damn but he looked good in her bed, she thought, sighing. And she liked knowing he was there when he was not out saving the world. In fact, she liked it a lot.

BRADY'S HAND was vibrating. It must have fallen asleep, he vaguely thought. It vibrated again and he roused himself, realizing he was the one that had fallen asleep. And the vibration was the pager clenched in his fist.

It took him a moment or two to figure out where he was, but an instant later he was sitting up in bed looking for her. He remembered lying across the bed while she rubbed his back...then it was all a blank. The bath towel he'd been wearing was tangled with the twisted bedsheets, so at some point he'd crawled under them. But as there was only one pillow, apparently he'd crawled in alone.

He glanced at the clock. Four in the morning. Where

was Erin? He looked around for his pants and found everything laid over a blue chair in the corner. He got up and pulled on his pants, then went out into the living room, his eyes rapidly adjusting to the dark. He spied her immediately, curled on the couch.

His pager hummed again and he swore silently and moved back to her bedroom, closing the door behind him before reaching for the phone. Five minutes later he was muttering under his breath and pulling on his clothes. Carrying his shoes and his holster, he moved back into the living room. He stopped by the couch and somehow ended up sitting on the coffee table staring at her while she slept. He debated carrying her to bed, but she looked quite comfortable all snuggled under a thick blanket and he didn't want to risk waking her. It was bad enough she'd had to give up her bed.

Still, he couldn't resist reaching out and lightly tracing her cheek with his finger. "What am I going to do about you?" he whispered. It was four in the morning and he was back on the job, with no idea when he'd be done again. And yet he was already planning on seeing her whenever that time came. If she'd let him.

He let his hand fall to his side. What kind of relationship was that going to be? He didn't have to ask, he knew. It would start out fine, with them both making compromises and not minding because they so badly wanted to see each other. But after a while it would be clear that she was making far more compromises than he was and the resentment would creep in. And finally that resentment would choke the life out of whatever had been between them. He'd never lived it himself, but he'd seen it happen often enough to know the drill.

He couldn't keep himself from touching her again. He really needed to hit the streets, go home and shave and get to the station. But he sat there, watching her sleep, wishing like hell he was a better man. Or at least a man who could offer her something real. Maybe they could have had something together, built something real. For the first time in his life, he honestly thought he wanted to try. It shocked him, the depth of this sudden need. He felt as though he barely knew her, and yet he felt he'd known her forever. *Maybe when you found the right person, you just knew*, he thought.

She rustled in her sleep, as if she somehow sensed his conflicting emotions. He made himself stand and move away from her. He should write her a note, but what would it say? He couldn't end it that way. Besides, she'd know where to find him when she realized he'd gone. She'd call him and he'd tell her then. Tell her the situation was impossible. Tell her he couldn't just play at this, that his heart was starting to get involved. No, he couldn't tell her that. But it didn't make it less true. He sighed and rubbed his hand over his face. He didn't know what in the hell he was going to tell her, he just knew he had to pull out right now, or they'd both end up being sorry for it. She'd understand.

He stopped at the door and looked back at her, feeling a tight ache seize his throat. Yeah, she'd understand. That's exactly why he was falling in love with her. She understood him far too well. Better than anyone. Enough that she'd let him go when he asked. "Damn."

ERIN STRETCHED and almost fell off the couch. "How on earth did I end up—" *Oh yeah.* She looked to the bedroom door. It was open. Her heart sank. He was gone.

She sat up and pulled the blanket around her. Something about the empty feeling—both in her apartment and inside herself—told her this emptiness was permanent. She got up and looked for a note or...or something to tell her that her gut instinct was wrong. No note. And she wasn't wrong. She knew it.

She climbed in the shower and tried to think about work. She'd signed a new client yesterday and another one was expecting a call from her later with a response to some of the questions he'd asked. She had to get her act together, meet with Gina to go over a few ideas, then get going on both these accounts. She knew she'd have to deal with Brady, too. But she didn't want to think about that right now. The bad feeling she had, despite the fact that he'd come to her last night, wouldn't go away.

She let the hot water beat down on her, thinking that he'd stood under this very spray the night before. Dammit, maybe she should have climbed in with him. Maybe if they'd made love again, she'd have felt more confident this morning. But he'd been in no shape to play, no matter that he would have tried anyway. She smiled despite the pain she felt squeezing her heart. "Stupid superhero."

She finished her shower, dried off then headed to the

closet. It was silly to be this hung up over him already. But it didn't feel like that. It felt as if she'd known him forever. And it wasn't because she'd known him as a kid. This went way deeper than that. They'd...connected somehow. And she was pretty sure he'd felt the same.

But that didn't change the fact that he was a cop with some strong ideas on commitment. Namely that those two things couldn't coexist. She yanked on some hose and grabbed the first suit she laid her hands on. She should let him go. She did understand his reservations. She had a truckload of them herself.

Her hands stilled in the act of buttoning her blazer. But dammit, maybe she didn't want to give him up. Maybe what they could have together was better than what they'd have apart. Maybe the good that came of sharing their lives would outweigh the tough parts they'd have to go alone. Maybe she was strong enough to be what he needed. At least she thought she might be. Enough to give it a try.

She sank into the chair in the corner of her room. But what if she failed? The pain would be...she didn't even want to go there. It would be the worst hell.

So what were her choices? Walk away and always wonder what if? Or fight and risk losing? She thought about calling Gina and hashing this out with her, but she didn't make a move for the phone. Instead she felt her lips slowly curve upward. Because she realized she'd already made her decision.

It simply wasn't in her to be a quitter. And maybe that was exactly what Brady needed in his life. Someone who wouldn't quit on him when things got tough. She knew it wouldn't be easy. She laughed harshly. "An understatement if there ever was one." But she also knew she wanted to be the one he stumbled home to. He'd respect her, respect that she had commitments, too. They'd be there for each other. She'd make him understand that. Stubborn, pigheaded man that he could be. One way or the other.

14

BRADY SHUFFLED OUT to his car. His eyes were gritty and burning, his stomach churning over the greasy take-out food he'd put in it, and his head throbbing with yet another tension headache. God, he loved his job.

He dragged himself behind the wheel and glanced over the running shoes lying on the passenger seat. So much for the jog he'd planned on today. He'd make it up tomorrow. Maybe. Right now all he wanted was—

Sleep. He'd been going to say sleep. Surely. But that wasn't the word that had popped into his mind. Erin had. Erin's smile, Erin's laugh, Erin's heavenly hands running all over his body.

Groaning, he turned the key in the ignition. No way was he intruding on her again tonight. He'd tried to call several times today but had never gotten in contact with her. That she hadn't returned his calls spoke volumes to him.

He was pulled from his dreary thoughts when his cell phone rang. He tugged it out of his pocket, all prepared to blister whoever it was that wanted even a second more of his time. That is, he was, until he noticed the number calling in. Erin's number. He was punch-

ing the answer button before his mind could come up
with all the reasons why he shouldn't.

"Hi."

"You sound beat," she said.

"Picked that up from one word, huh? Good ears."

"I also have good hands. You sound like you could
use them right about now."

His body clamored for him to take her up on that offer. His mind, however, pushed at him to do the right
thing. "Listen, Erin—"

"You're tired, you need rest, I know. Why don't we
meet at Jimmy's tomorrow. Will you have some time?"

She didn't badger him about the case, even though
he knew she was probably dying for details. He appreciated that. *Do the right thing. She doesn't deserve to be
strung along.* "Yeah, I'll make time." The right thing
was telling her in person, he told himself. That was the
only reason he'd agreed. Not because he had to see her
again one last time. "I'll call you in the morning if
that's okay."

"That would be fine." There was a pause, then,
"Brady, listen, I know you're uncomfortable with
where this is going." She stopped and laughed, but
there was no humor in it. "I promised I wasn't going to
do this over the phone."

Brady's heart pounded. So she was going to end it
first? He should be relieved. There would be no scene,
no problem. Just two adults who realized things were
getting out of hand. A clean break. He should have
given her more credit, just told her straight out. But he
hadn't.

And he knew why. His hands tightened on the steering wheel. *Don't say the words, Erin*, was the first thought that ran through his head. That was not the reaction of a man who was ready to end it.

She blew out a long breath and Brady heard the vulnerability in her tone when she continued. "I know you have a million reasons, almost all of them good ones, for not wanting to pursue this...thing between us."

"Thing?" His pulse continued to hammer.

"The plan's not working, Brady."

"The plan." Was she saying goodbye or...or not?

She swore under her breath. "Yeah, you know. The plan I had. Where we just—" She didn't finish.

If he hadn't been a ball of nerves, he'd have been amused at her inability to name their liaison. She was such an enjoyable contradiction. "Where we just... release?"

She sighed, but there was as much remembered pleasure in it as there was frustration. "Yeah," she said weakly. "That plan." She cleared her throat, shored up her resolve. "At least for me it isn't—it won't work." She spoke in a rush now. "I know I told you it would just be for fun. No feelings involved," she hurried on. "Well. I screwed up."

"Are you saying you want to end it?"

"No!" she blurted immediately. "I mean, I don't want to, but I can't continue without letting you know that, well, it's not the same now. At least not for me."

She wasn't breaking it off! Suddenly he didn't feel as tired anymore. In fact, he felt downright energized.

"So now this...thing between us is a different...thing?" He probably shouldn't tease her, but he simply couldn't help himself. "Just what kind of *thing* is it now, Erin?"

"You're starting to irritate me."

"Then why are you smiling?"

"I'm not smiling." She broke off, then he heard her mutter something under her breath. "Okay, so I'm smiling. Dammit. How do you do that to me?"

The same way you do it to me. "I want to hear more about this thing we shouldn't be having but are anyway."

"Well, I didn't want to use the R word and scare you off completely," she responded, sounding more relaxed, too.

He liked this give-and-take they fell into so easily. Her dry humor and sharp wit, his unhurried comebacks. That kind of byplay aroused him as always. But it was also...soothing. Yeah, soothing. Like no matter how screwed up the rest of the world was, everything was right in his world when he heard that note in her voice.

"The R word, huh?" He let his head rest against the back of the seat. "R. You mean, as in relationship?"

"That would be the one. Did saying it leave a bitter taste in your mouth?"

He laughed. "Surprisingly, no. No, it didn't." The tensions of the day slowly ebbed away. He couldn't escape the notion that as long as she kept talking, it would all be okay. How had he ever survived without her easing his life this way? "So, you said almost all of my million reasons for not doing this were good ones. Which ones weren't?"

"The ones that say that just because the odds are against something, you automatically quit without trying." She paused for a moment, and they both sobered. "Unless you never wanted to try in the first place."

"I don't think that's the case," he said quietly.

"That's what I was hoping."

He took a long breath at the same time she did. "You make it sound easy, Erin. You make me want to take you up on that offer of a backrub. And everything else that comes with it. Badly. But I also know that I could be yanked away from you again at any second. I don't want it—want us—to go there. To where you resent me. My job." He heaved a sigh. "As much as I don't want to, maybe we should listen to those million reasons. Maybe those odds are the odds for a reason. Maybe we shouldn't be so willing to add to that statistic."

"And maybe you should give me a little more credit than you do."

"Meaning what?"

"Meaning I'm a grown woman who is perfectly aware that she's entering into a relationship with a man dedicated to a job that doesn't respect family or relationships or anything else except justice." She let him think about that for a moment, then softly said, "Maybe this will lead to the pain and heartache that you see happening to other cops around you. But you can't tell me they are all miserable, that there aren't relationships that work."

"No, but—"

"But do you want to find out about us? Maybe we'll be the other statistic. Or would you rather always wonder if I was right about this too?"

His lips quirked at that, but his tone remained even. "I don't want us to end up enemies. That's what I don't want."

"I don't want that either."

"How do we make sure that doesn't happen?"

"I don't think we get to try for one without risking the other. We can hope we'll handle whatever comes our way the best we can, like adults. But I can't make you any promises. Except one."

Brady's throat tightened. "Which is?"

"That I'll always be honest with you. If I can't handle it, I'll tell you. If we can find a way to work around the problems, we will. If not..." She didn't finish.

"I'm starting to see why you're doing so well with your business."

"I drive a hard bargain, O'Keefe. I'm going to expect the same commitment from you. Uh-oh. I went and used the C word. Did I blow the deal?"

"No," he said, chuckling. "No, you didn't blow the deal."

She blew out a long, shaky breath and Brady swore he heard her whisper, "Thank God."

And that was the crux of her appeal. A sturdy defense, a shield of confidence, and underneath it all a heart that could still be just as insecure as his.

"So we're officially doing the R word now?" he asked.

"Yes!" She quickly cleared her throat and sounded calmer when she added, "I, um, I guess we are. Yes. Yes, we definitely are."

"What's that pounding noise?"

"Pounding noise?"

He grinned. "Yeah. The pounding noise that just stopped. Right when I asked you what the pounding noise was."

"Oh. That noise."

"Yeah. What was it?"

"My, um, my feet. On the coffee table."

Brady's grin threatened to bust to a laugh. He held it back. "Is something wrong? Foot fall asleep?"

It didn't take long for her to regroup. "You're really enjoying this, aren't you?"

"Isn't that what people in relationships are supposed to do? Enjoy one another?"

"Not at the other's expense."

"Oh. So, I'm not supposed to enjoy that you were doing a victory dance on your coffee table over closing the deal? This relationship thing is new to me, so you'll have to cut me a little slack."

"I'm beginning to wish I'd never taught you the R word. And you'll get no slack. Not from me. Not ever."

"Good," he said, this time very serious. "I'm counting on that."

"We'll see."

"Yeah, I guess we will." He was officially getting involved with Terror Maloney. Hell, he was already involved. Over-his-head involved. "Is that backrub offer

still valid?" She said nothing. "Erin, are you still
there?"

"I'm considering."

He laughed. "Considering what?"

"Whether I should use my hands...or my feet."

"You can use whatever you want on me." He gen-
tled his voice. He wasn't teasing her now. "I just want
to feel you touch me again, Erin."

She breathed audibly. "You might be better at this
relationship thing than you give yourself credit for."

"So that is a yes?"

"Damn right it is. So hurry."

ERIN FLOATED in to work the next morning. Brady
hadn't left until five that morning. A beeper-free night.
She was going to have to get him to bring a change of
clothes next time. She grinned and danced across the
room to her desk. There was going to be a next time!

She fell blissfully into her chair, then winced and
moved to a more comfortable position. "The man is a
superhero in more way than one," she murmured. She
just wasn't used to so much...activity. Her body and all
those wonderful muscles she'd discovered she had
would simply have to catch up. And soon, if she had
anything to say about it.

"Boy, if ever the cat looked like she'd eaten the pro-
verbial canary." Gina leaned on the open door to Erin's
office. "Or should I say Detective Canary?"

Erin just laughed. Gina made a beeline to Erin's
desk, hopped on the corner of it, legs already crossed.
"Spill."

"You know what they say about the curious cat."

Gina waved her off. "Oh that. I have at least…" She looked up to the ceiling as if mentally calculating, then grinned back at Erin. "Four or five lives left." She leaned forward. "So tell me everything. From the look on your face, it will be worth losing another one."

"Gina," she warned.

"Erin," Gina whined. "Okay, okay. Just one detail. But make it juicy. Jeremy did the dump-n-run on me last night, so I need cheering up."

"Who is Jeremy?"

"Exactly. Now tell me. Please?"

"I swear, Gina, you know, maybe if you gave a guy some credit for having brains and not just—"

"Brawn?" She sighed lustily. "Jeremy did have brawn."

Erin gave her a look. "I'm just saying that there are men out there who are worthy."

Gina swooned. "Oh my God. She's in love."

"I didn't say that."

"You didn't have to, girlfriend."

Erin grew thoughtful. "I'm not in love with him, Gina. But I could be." She pictured Brady as he'd been last night. On the phone, in her shower, in her bed, in her arms. Smiling, laughing, groaning, climaxing. Looking into her eyes like no one ever had. "Yeah, I could be," she said softly.

Gina sobered. "Whoa."

Erin laughed gently. "Oh yeah. Big whoa."

"He's a cop. You said—"

"I know what I said. But we've talked about it and

we'll deal with it as realistically as we can. I know it won't be easy. But I don't want anyone else. I've never wanted anyone like I want this man."

"A man who puts himself in the line of fire as a part of his job."

Erin shuddered. "Don't remind me. But, as much as I hate that part, what he does is a huge part of who he is. I wouldn't want one without the other."

Gina shrugged and nodded. "I guess we can all go at any time, when you think about it."

"I knew I loved you for a good reason. Yes, you are exactly right. I won't give up what we might have for what might, or might never, happen."

"Are you afraid?"

Erin looked straight at her best friend. "Terrified. But also excited, exhilarated, alive. It's worth the fear."

Gina slid off the desk and came around to give her a hug. "Well then, I hope the best for you. Both of you."

"Thanks." She thought she might cry, and it was too wonderful a day to get teary, so she purposely looked at the stack of folders on her desk. "Did you look at the proposal for Davidson?"

Gina suspiciously wiped at her eyes, but managed to regain her professional demeanor as well. "Actually, that's what I came in here for. It looks good, but I think your projections are a bit enthusiastic." She dipped her chin and said slyly, "Must be all that exhilaration making your glasses a bit too rosy."

"Here she goes with the jokes already. I'll go back over it before we meet this afternoon."

"Works for me," she said as she sailed out the door.

"Hey," Erin called her back. When Gina stuck her head back in the door, she grinned wickedly and said, "Four times. In one night. There is your one juicy detail."

Gina fanned herself. "Remind me not to ask you for any more." She walked away and Erin heard her grumble, "Damn Jesse for up and leaving—"

"Jeremy," Erin called out. "I thought his name was Jeremy."

Gina went on without missing a beat. "Damn Jeremy for leaving me in my time of need." She raised her voice so Erin could clearly hear her. "And I do mean need!"

Erin was laughing as she flipped open the Davidson folder. Her phone rang and she picked it up, her mind on the projection sheet in front of her. "Mahoney and Briggs, Erin Mahoney speaking."

"Erin."

"Brady! Hi." She was surprised and happy to hear from him, so it took her a second to process the tone in his voice. "What's wrong?"

"This whole Sanderson thing is being blown wide open. There's been another homicide, a zoning commissioner this time. We think we know who did it, but I can't—" He broke off and swore as there was shouting and someone barking his name in the background. "Listen, I have to run, but I'll probably be late tonight. Don't wait up. I'll call later if I can. I'm sorry."

"It's okay, really. I under—" She suddenly realized she was talking to dead air. "Stand," she finished, hanging up the receiver. She was disappointed, but glad he'd thought to call and tell her. So this is what it was going to be like. She would sit and wait and worry while he was out risking God knew what. But honestly, she would worry about him anyway. At least now she knew he'd call, or come to see her when it was all said and done. And she wanted that.

Her thoughts switched to the murder. Who else had been killed and who'd done it? Maybe they would finally be able to nail the Han family for Sanderson's murder. Maybe Bradford Pitts's too. She got up to go tell Gina. Maybe it would be on the news.

She never got past her office door. Gina was standing in the hallway, her arms being forcefully held behind her back, a very large, very black gun being held to her head.

"Hi, Erin," he said.

Erin's gaze darted from Gina's terrified face, to the man holding her captive. "You?"

15

"Yes, it's me." Todd Fletcher pressed the gun harder into Gina's temple, discouraging her from wiggling.

"But why?" Erin was in shock. She'd known Todd was a weasel, but she hadn't thought him a murderous weasel. *Think, Erin, think.* "You'll harm the mayor's re-election campaign. You know he wouldn't want you to do this."

Todd laughed, then his voice caught almost like a sob. "Don't you think I know that?" He cackled again, raising the hairs on Erin's arms with the half-mad sound of it. "But it's too late now."

There was a sudden banging on the front doors of the office. "Police! Open the door now!"

Erin jumped, but realized quickly that Todd was not going to give up easily. He didn't seem surprised at all by the sudden presence of the police. He pulled Gina's head back. "Don't make a sound. I will do all the talking." He stared at Erin until she finally nodded, then he called out, "This is Todd Fletcher. I demand to see Detective Brady O'Keefe. I won't talk to anyone else. I have two hostages, one of them is Erin Mahoney. You tell him that. If you try to enter this room, I will take them both out." He let out that half laugh, half cry again and added, "It's not like I have anything to lose."

Then he snarled and jabbed Gina again. "So don't test me!"

Erin swallowed hard at the mention of Brady's name. What did Todd want with him? She was still trying to come to terms with the fact that Todd was somehow involved in a murder. It was too coincidental that he'd showed up just after Brady had called. She tried to take a calming breath. Brady had said they thought they knew who did it and the police were outside the door.

Still, how was Todd involved in Sanderson's death? She couldn't see any possible connection. What about Bradford Pitts? Had Todd been so worried about what the reporter was digging up that he'd actually killed him, too? Even seeing him standing in front of her, obviously pushed over the edge of despair, she couldn't imagine it.

"Todd," she said quietly. He swung his wild-eyed gaze back to her. "Why don't you let Gina go? We can't go anywhere or do anything. You could lock us in my office until—" She faltered. She didn't want Brady here. Didn't want him to walk into this. "Until this is resolved. We're still hostages."

Todd shook his head. "I might be desperate, but I'm not stupid. You'll stay right where you are."

"Fine, fine. Just let Gina come over and stand with me, okay? You don't need to hurt her, she didn't do anything. She has nothing to do with any of this."

Erin was still trying to figure out what *she* had to do with this. She was officially out of Todd's hair, so why threaten her like this? Then it hit her. He only wanted

Brady. He knew they were seeing each other and that Brady would come because he was holding her hostage.

In all the potential dating-a-cop scenarios she'd run through her mind, it had always been her coping with the danger Brady put himself in. Never once did she consider that she would now be a weakness to him, a vulnerable spot that could be exploited. She was worried about her safety, but now she was going to be used against him, to possibly put him in danger. Dammit, didn't he risk enough?

She felt her throat close over. Reason one million and one for not falling in love with a cop. Or, more specifically, not letting a cop fall for her. She couldn't do this to him, affect his job this way. No way was he going to be put in more danger because she'd forced him to give this relationship a try.

She eyed Todd, recalling how he'd reacted to her that day in the hallway. She had no idea if he was too strung out now to react to her again, but damn if she wasn't going to try. The police hadn't made any other movement in the hall, which meant they were probably getting Brady. She had to end this before he got here and did something foolish to save her. And she knew he would. She told herself it was his integrity that would make him risk life and limb, that he'd do it for any civilian in danger. And she was right...but she also couldn't stop thinking about the Brady O'Keefe who'd been in her bed this morning. She blinked hard against the tears that suddenly threatened. She saw his face, his unwavering gaze before he kissed her goodbye, promising her he'd return to her as soon as he could. The man who might be falling in love with her.

The man she realized now she'd already fallen in love with.

She swallowed hard against the ache in her throat, turning her attention once again to Todd. This time she stood a little straighter, shoulders back a little, chest a bit more prominently displayed. Gina's eyes widened in disbelief and she knew her best friend had seen right through her plan. She only hoped Todd didn't.

She forced a slow, sinuous smile onto her face. "Todd," she said softly. He jerked his gaze to hers, his eyes widening in confusion at the expression on her face. She moved swiftly, hoping to capitalize on that confusion. "You know I'm friends with O'Keefe." She daringly took another step closer to him. "I'm sure if you explain all this to me, I can help you out." Another step. "I mean, I know we had our disagreements with the mayor's campaign, but I know you don't hold that against me. After all, you got your way in the end." She smiled even more broadly and took another step forward, hoping her shaking legs weren't obvious. "Well, where Detective O'Keefe is concerned, let's just say I can probably get my way. In the end." She purposely did not look at Gina's terrified face. "I think you know what I mean."

Todd swallowed hard and sweat popped out on his forehead.

"I'll even let you take me hostage instead of Gina. O'Keefe will be a lot more likely to listen if I'm directly threatened, don't you think?"

"Erin," Gina whispered viciously, but Erin kept her gaze firmly on Todd.

She stretched a trembling hand toward him. "Come on now, let her go." She got him to look her in the eyes. He was scared, but they weren't the eyes of a killer. At least she didn't think they were. "Let her go. You can have me."

The phones began ringing, she heard her cell phone ringing, too. *Brady*. She focused on Todd, blocking everything else out. "Come on. You do want me, don't you, Todd?"

Todd was sweating profusely now, confusion mixed with fear in his eyes. "I just want to explain," he said, the anger in his tone edging toward a whine. "I can explain."

"I know you can." Erin saw his grip on the gun relax a bit. "And I want you to tell me all of it. I know we can make them understand. I'm good at that, Todd. I'm good at making people understand a bad situation isn't what it seems. That's what I do for a living, right?" She kept talking, watching the gun in her peripheral vision. "So why don't we go talk this over, then I can talk to O'Keefe when he gets here and it will all be over. He'll understand whatever I tell him. You did a smart thing coming to me first."

Todd's eyes clouded then and she thought he might break down and cry. "I thought I had it under control," he said, half whimpering, half raging. "I didn't kill him. I only wanted proof, I didn't kill him."

"Of course you didn't," she said, but inside she was breathing a major sigh of relief. She hadn't thought he was a killer. A weasel yes, but not a killer. But she had no idea what had happened to bring him to this point. Thankfully it looked as if he was starting to lose his willpower to continue. She tugged at Gina's arm, again keeping her gaze on Todd. "Gina, why don't you sit down right there and let Todd and me talk this over."

Todd's arm began to relax as Gina slid out of his grasp, then suddenly he snapped to attention, his eyes clearing as if he was just now realizing what was happening. "No! Wait!"

But Gina was already free. "I'm sitting right here," she said shakily. "Not doing a thing. Minding my own business."

Todd swung his suspicious gaze—and the gun—to Erin. "If she moves—"

"She won't move." Erin worked hard to put the knowing smile back on her face. It had been hard enough when the gun was pointed at Gina. It was downright petrifying now that it was pointed at her. "We don't need her, Todd. You only need me."

He wiped his face with his free hand. "You can't help me. You wanted Henley to talk to the press. I won't talk to the press. They'll kill me if this gets out before I talk to O'Keefe. He has to listen, he has to believe me."

"No press. You're right. You and I both have experience in how to explain things to people. That's why the mayor hired you. Surely together we can make them understand." She stepped closer to him, keeping her eyes on him...and off the gun. "Who wants to hurt you, Todd? The Hans?" She'd made a wild guess and instantly saw she'd hit it on the first try.

He swallowed hard several times, the sweat pouring down his face now. He darted a quick look around, as if there might be someone tucked in the corner listening. "They...they—" Tears clogged his throat. "I just wanted information, I never intended anyone to get hurt. Or...or killed. I didn't kill him. I should have listened when they killed Pitts, but I didn't kill the zoning guy. They're making it look like I did, but it wasn't my fault."

"You know they killed Bradford?" *Why the hell didn't you tell the police then?* she wanted to demand. But hurling accusations at him was the last thing she needed to do. Besides, he wasn't listening to her anyway.

"They tried to blackmail Morton and he ended up dead. They shut Pitts up for good." He was trembling now. "I should have listened, but I thought I had it under control. Don't you understand?" He was shrieking now, but almost in tears at the same time. His tone suddenly turned pleading. "I couldn't give them what they wanted, but that doesn't make it my fault." He was breathing heavily now. "No one will believe that. They'll think I killed them all." He started crying in earnest now. "Oh God, they'll kill me anyway, what difference does it make?"

Erin thought about trying to take the gun from him, but she wasn't that sure she could. And with Gina on the floor, she couldn't risk the gun going off. "The police can protect you, Todd. That information you have is power. You of all people know how powerful the person with the information is. Use it, Todd. Use it to help yourself."

She wasn't even certain he was listening to her anymore. The gun wavered in his grip. She was trying to decide whether to go for it, when someone pounded on the door again.

"Fletcher! It's Detective O'Keefe."

Todd panicked and grabbed Erin, turning her back to his chest and swinging the gun around in front of her. She probably shouldn't have fought him, but she panicked too and reacted instinctively to being grabbed at. She kicked her spiked heel swiftly back and up, landing a good jab right between Todd's legs. He cried out, his gun hand swinging wide. She chopped at his arm, hoping he'd drop the weapon. The gun went flying, but not before one shot rang out.

Erin dived at Todd just as he and Gina dived for the flying gun. The door to the office burst open a second later and the foyer was immediately filled with police officers, led by Brady, each of them with guns drawn. They all came stumbling to a stop as they took in the situation.

Gina was leaning back against the wall, the gun dangling from her fingers. Erin was straddling a hysterically sobbing Todd, pinning him to the floor. She smiled up at Brady. "About time you got here."

The ferocious look on his face almost did her in. It was only by the edge of her wits that she'd pulled off that last line. But she didn't want him to see how terrified she was, or just how close to dying she'd come.

Several uniformed police officers stepped in just

then to control Todd, while two others helped her up. It was all she could do not to fling herself at Brady and sob hysterically herself. It took every remaining drop of control she had to maintain the banter she'd instigated. "Superwoman to the rescue. What a team, huh?"

Brady barked out several orders to the surrounding throng of cops, but his gaze never once left hers. She knew better than to trust her legs to so much as move one step. She'd crumple to the floor for sure. The adrenaline that had pumped by the gallon into her system was rushing right back out again and just as swiftly.

Gina stumbled to her just then and caught her in a tight bear hug. "Oh my God, Erin, you were amazing. You saved my life."

Brady forced his attention away from Gina clinging to an apparently unharmed Erin so he could oversee Todd's handcuffing and removal from the scene. His mind was a jumbled mess of instincts, some job related, but most of them personal. He finally asked the remaining officers to step outside, before turning back to face them.

He wasn't ready to deal with Erin yet, his emotions were too raw and close to the surface. He was here as a cop, not as her lover, and it took all his control and focus to remember that at the moment. "Are you okay?" The question was directed to Gina.

She nodded shakily. "Yeah. Just scared." She looked to Erin, then back to Brady. "I'll be out in the hallway."

"We'll need to ask you some questions, take a statement about what happened. You'll have to decide if you want to press charges against Fletcher. You might want to call an attorney for advice. That's up to you." Brady helped her to the door. "You want to see a doctor first? Talk to a counselor?"

She shook her head. "No, I'll be okay." She paused at the door and looked past Brady's shoulder at Erin, then back at him. "She kicked ass in there, Detective. You can be proud of her. She really held up." She looked directly at him. "She did it for you, you know, to keep you safe."

"Me?"

"Yeah. Detective Hunk was coming to the rescue. I know her and she'd hate thinking she could be used to put you in any kind of danger. So don't let her do anything stupid, like try and break it off with you. Because she's the best thing you'll ever have." She moved out in the hall. "Don't you screw that up either. Instead of looking like you want to wring her neck, you should be kissing her right now and thanking God that bullet didn't hit anything more important than my favorite watercolor. Remember, she didn't ask to have a gun shoved in her face. She handled it and we're fine. That's all that matters."

Gina slid by him, and Brady turned back to the office where Erin was leaning against the wall. As soon as she realized he was back, she stood up straight, adopted her casual little I-can-handle-anything smile. Brady flashed to that moment when he'd heard the gunshot. It felt as if his whole life had ended in that one instant. And then he'd come bursting through the door, only to find her handling the bad guy and tossing off smart-ass comments. And Gina had been dead right. He'd been torn between throttling her and yanking her into his arms where he could make sure she was all right.

He'd done neither of those things. He'd frozen. Trapped somewhere between being cop and lover, not prepared to be both at the same time. Never before had he allowed anything to interfere with the process. Until now. So he'd reverted to cop mode, processing the scene and barking orders. It was what he did, what he knew best. Only this time he did it to keep himself from thinking about what had really happened here today. And what could have happened.

"Brady?"

He realized he was standing there in a haze. She was frowning now, looking concerned. Well, it was about damn time. She hadn't looked all that concerned when she had a potential murderer pinned beneath her. But she looked worried now. Because of him.

She did it for you, to keep you safe.

Gina's words rang in his ears, almost as loudly as that single gunshot.

Erin crossed the room and took hold of his arms. "What's wrong?"

He tugged free, the anger coming seemingly out of nowhere. "What's wrong? Wrong?" He clamped his jaw down, hoping to also clamp the sudden surge of temper down along with it. He knew better than anyone that it was just a delayed reaction to the stress and fear of what he'd walked into moments ago. But knowing that didn't seem to give him the strength to stop the words from flowing. "What the hell did you think you were doing? You could have gotten yourself killed. Or Gina. Or even Fletcher, damn his sniveling, cowardly little weasel-ass hide."

Erin's eyes widened, then narrowed. She carefully folded her arms in front of her. "I thought I was doing my best to save my life and Gina's. You'll have to pardon me if I didn't follow police procedure. I'm only an ignorant civilian."

He stepped closer. "You knew the hall was filled with police officers, trained to handle things like this. You also knew damn well I was on my way."

Now temper snapped into her eyes as well. "Yes, I did. But that gun wasn't being pointed at the police officers in the hall. And it wasn't pointed at you. And excuse me for not wanting it ever to be pointed at you." She poked him in the chest. "Yes, I knew you were coming and it galled me that I could be used against you. I simply refused to tolerate that. So I did what I thought I had to do. And if you don't like it, well, tough beans, Detective."

She shoved past him and stalked to the hall. "I'll have someone drive me downtown so I can file my statement."

"Don't you want to know what happened? Why Todd was here?" It was the first thing he thought of to say, because he knew damn well her curiosity would keep her here. Hopefully long enough for his head to stop spinning and for him to get a grip and sort through this.

Naturally she didn't follow his plan.

"I think I put together most of it. I'm sure someone at the station will fill me in on the rest. After all, as I proved today, I'm pretty good at getting people to tell me things when I set my..." She deliberately paused, then finished with, "Mind to it."

"What the hell do you mean by that?" So much for reining in his temper. "What exactly went on in here?"

"Guess you'll have to read it in my report." Then she was gone.

Brady stormed after her, but stopped short when he caught Gina's folded arms and accusing glare.

He watched as she stomped over to Erin, then he turned back inside the office, motioning several uniforms in with him. This was not the time or place to deal with this. He had a job to do. And yet he knew the instant Erin left the building.

Hell, this whole place smelled like Erin's perfume. He should have gone downtown with her, stood by her while she gave her statement. When the adrenaline and shock wore off she'd be shaky and scared. He knew all the signs, all the aftereffects. He was beginning to feel them himself.

"Detective?"

He turned to the uniform waiting for his next order. Gina was with Erin. She'd be okay. But for the first time ever he resented the job for coming first. He looked once more to the door, then turned back. "Yeah, I'm coming."

16

ERIN WAS JUST TYING the belt to her bathrobe when the doorbell rang. She froze, her heart speeding up, then just as quickly made herself calm down. It was just Gina. Not a crazy man with a gun.

And not Brady.

She hadn't seen him at the station at all. He had left a brief, terse message on her machine, telling her he'd call her later tonight if he could. She wasn't sure she'd be ready to deal with him even then. Her feelings were still ragged, which was why she'd called Gina and begged her to come over. They'd been separated at the station and she'd missed getting the chance to speak to her again. She really needed someone to talk to right now, and a police guidance counselor was not what she had in mind.

Reporters had clogged the front of the police station and, according to the news on the radio, they were piled up on the steps of city hall as well. She'd taken the back way out and was thankful there wasn't anyone parked at her door when she got home. She'd told herself she wasn't disappointed that Brady hadn't been parked on her doorstep, either.

She peeked through the eyehole, prepared to see Gina's smiling face, only to spy Brady standing there instead. She pulled her hand away from the chain, her heart speeding right back up again.

She had fallen, and fallen hard, for Brady O'Keefe. Occupational hazards and all. In fact, having done a lot of thinking on it, she'd come to the conclusion that she'd be a damn good partner for him in that respect. She could more than handle her own in difficult situations. She wasn't the clingy, needy sort. She could be there for him and not fall apart just because he was called out on an assignment. Or two, or ten dozen. She wasn't fooling herself that it would be easy, but she was prepared to work hard to make this relationship work.

That was the pro argument. It was the con argument she had yet to come to terms with. As much as she'd like to think of herself as an asset to him, as a woman and lover, as a friend and confidante...she also knew now she was a liability to him. She represented a weakness in his armor. Not just as a potential hostage. She realized her involvement in this case was a rarity, not likely to be repeated. But it had brought home to her that simply by being involved with him, she commanded a certain amount of his concentration, thereby diverting that focus from the job. He wasn't as safe if his attention wasn't completely on the job. And she'd seen firsthand today how well he'd coped with mixing their personal relationship with his job.

"Erin?"

She jumped, then looked out the eyehole again. He was raking his hand through his already rumpled hair. His face was set, but she saw the fatigue lining his eyes.

Fatigue and worry. And she knew he was worried about her.

Pro versus con. Safety versus risk. Love versus integrity. What should she do?

She slid the chain free and opened the door.

BRADY STOOD THERE and stared at her. As usual, all his carefully planned words disappeared in a blink. Her hair was in a damp tangle around her shoulders, making her eyes look huge and luminous. Her robe was so thick and tightly belted it made her look slender and fragile by comparison. The urge to pull her into his arms, apologize for the appalling situation she'd found herself in today and for the way he'd handled it, promise her he'd never ever let anything happen to her again, was so strong he had to curl his fingers inward and force his feet to remain planted where they were. Because he couldn't promise he could keep her safe. He'd learned that the hard way today. He couldn't wrap her in a cocoon of safety and she'd never want that anyway.

"Hi," she said softly.

"Hi." He couldn't stop looking at her. His entire body was one giant knot of need, and the need had grown way past sexual. "Can I come in?"

She seemed to be in a haze too, because she quickly stepped back as if suddenly realizing they were just standing in the doorway. "Sure, sure." She motioned to the living room. "I'm going to change. Help yourself to a beer or whatever. I'll only be a minute. Just, um, I'll be right back." She was babbling and she almost tripped—twice—on her way to the bedroom.

He should be heartened that he was not the only one feeling mixed up and confused. But he wasn't. He realized now that he'd been half hoping he'd show up and she'd simply present him with another one of her nifty plans and he'd go along with it and everything would be all fine and dandy. Problems solved. At least temporarily.

He took a beer out of the fridge and swallowed half of it in one long pull. Then he set the bottle on the counter and promptly forgot about it when her bedroom door opened. She came out in jeans and a large gray sweatshirt, her hair making damp marks on the shoulders. Her feet were still bare, as was her face. And he thought she was the most beautiful woman on the planet.

"I need to warn you," she said. "Gina is on her way over, so if you think it would be better, maybe we should delay our little talk."

He fought the urge to smile. She'd sounded almost hopeful about putting this off. He should be agreeing and getting the hell out of there, except he just now realized he knew what he wanted to say. And it wasn't goodbye. Not now, not ever. Looking into her eyes, his heart swelled as if everything was suddenly right in his world because she was in it. And it was. Why he'd been wanting to fight that was lost on him at that moment. He only knew he had to tell her and he wasn't leaving here until he did. But first things first. "Gina isn't coming over," he said, his mind already racing ahead.

"Oh?"

"She, uh, she called me. Said you needed to talk. As it happens, I needed to talk to you, too, so we figured maybe we'd just talk to each other and leave her out of it."

"You figured that, did you?" Erin paced the length of the room, then back again. "I suppose I should be surprised, or at least angry." She stopped and blew out a long breath. "But I'm not."

He didn't need her plan, he had his own plan. A long-term plan. He felt ridiculously lighthearted, like singing, shouting even. "So, I'm officially staying?"

"Officially, yes. Only I reserve the right to eject you from the game at any time I see fit." She shot him that dry smile. "Home field advantage."

Brady sat on the couch, deciding right then and there this evening wasn't going to end with him being ejected. No matter what he had to do to convince her. He leaned back and tried to relax. "I'll try and behave."

She perched at the other end of the couch and tucked her feet beneath her. "You do that."

They stared at each other for a long moment while Brady tried to decide the best way to do this. His palms were sweating. Hell, even the soles of his feet were sweating. He'd never felt this way before, much less done anything about it. This was so important, it was so vital that he get it right. He didn't dare screw it up. After all, he was staring at his whole future.

"Okay, okay, so I'm asking," she said in exasperation.

That got his attention. *She* was going to propose? And like that? Wait, this was *his* plan! "What did you say?"

Erin folded her arms. "What's going to happen to Todd? What exactly did he do? Did the Hans kill that zoning commissioner? And Sanderson and Bradford? Are they in custody? Was Todd charged with anything?"

Brady was so taken off guard his mouth fell open. He was sitting there sweating bullets over planning their future together and she was thinking about Todd Fletcher? "You mean you don't know?"

She narrowed her eyes. "Don't play coy. I tried, but everyone at the station told me it would have to come from you. Not that this is a shock to you, I'm sure."

"And you think I put them up to it?" He shook his head. "Much as I'd like to take credit, I have to say they were simply following procedure. But I wish I had that kind of power sometimes." He couldn't help it, he grinned. "So your infamous wiles failed you, huh?"

"Oh, ha ha ha." But she couldn't maintain a straight face either. "Yes, they did. Dammit." She had to look away for a moment to keep from laughing. "So, if you're done gloating now, tell me what happened. I know it's all over the news, but I wanted to hear it from you."

Now he frowned, concerned. "Have the reporters been bothering you?"

"I turned my phone off and left the machine to take messages. But don't worry, I'll deal with that."

And he knew she would, handily. It was one of the many things he respected about her, her ability to stand on her own two feet.

"Right now I just want to know exactly why I had a gun pointed at me today."

Brady felt his heart drop straight to his toes. Just hearing her say that brought it all back for him. And from the fear that flashed through her eyes, it had for her, too.

"I really want to explain all this calmly and in detail," he said, working to keep his voice even. "I want to tell you what I thought about it then, and what it made me realize in how I feel about you and all the plans I want to make now that I've figured it all out." He stood up and moved to her end of the couch. "Only right at this moment I can't think straight, much less explain anything to you, until I do this."

He tugged her up and into his arms, then exhaled deeply when she moved willingly into them and held him as tightly as he held her. "I should have done this earlier today. I'm sorry. I've never been so—" His throat closed over and it took him a moment. "I didn't know how to react, and I—" His voice caught again and he buried his face in her hair. "Thank God, you're okay," he whispered.

"I'm okay, Brady." She pushed her hands into his hair and pulled his head down to hers. "I'm okay." She kissed him lightly on the lips, then actually started to move back.

As if he had any plans on letting her go. Ever. He tugged her right back against him and kissed her back, only there was nothing light about it. She resisted for a millisecond, then a moan of pleasure rose from deep in her throat—or maybe it was from his—and she leaned fully into him.

When he could finally bring himself to let her mouth go, he still held her tightly against him. "I know you can take care of yourself, Erin," he said roughly. "I respect that about you and I don't want you to think I don't." He pulled back and looked into her eyes. "But please God don't ever do anything like that ever again."

"Trust me, it wasn't anything I wanted to do." Then she blinked hard and he saw moisture gather in her eyes. "I didn't want you to do anything foolish to try and save us."

"That's my job." His lips quirked. "Not the foolish part, but the lifesaving part." He kissed her gently, almost reverently, on the lips. "You have to trust that I know what I'm doing and I would never risk anything foolishly."

"Including yourself?" she asked doubtfully.

"Of course." He'd said it automatically, even knowing he'd give his life for hers in a heartbeat.

She shook her head, a smile lifting the corners of her mouth. "You don't have any clue, do you?"

Now he was confused. "About what?"

"How did you feel today when you heard that gunshot?"

His stomach pitched hard just hearing her ask. "It was the single worst moment of my life."

She nodded. "Exactly."

"You lost me."

"You didn't want anything to happen to me."

"Of course I didn't."

"Or Gina."

It took him a moment to shift gears. "Of course."

"Right. Because you'd put your life on the line for any citizen in danger, that is part of your job."

He nodded, having no idea where she was leading him.

"But can you honestly say your fear for my life being in jeopardy was equal to that of your fear for Gina, or any citizen in jeopardy?"

"That's not a fair question. You know I wouldn't compromise—"

"I know you wouldn't. That's not what I asked."

He looked into her eyes as realization dawned. "Yes, I was more worried than usual because you were involved. Terrified, in fact."

"Than maybe you can understand that I was operating with that same level of fear. I no more wanted to put you in the path of a bullet than you did me."

"I guess the fact that I'm trained for situations like that doesn't make a difference."

She shook her head. "Not one tiny bit."

He stroked her face. "I didn't say this because I was too terrified and angry at the time, but I was—am—very proud of how you handled yourself in there today." She shuddered and he pulled her close again. "I just don't ever want either of us to face that kind of situation again."

She did pull out of his arms now. "And that is where I was going with this." She moved away when he reached for her, wrapping her arms around her waist instead. "You need to maintain that edge, that focus, in what you do, to keep you as alert as possible at all times." She paced away from him, then back again. "I...I don't want to be a liability to that. I don't mean I think I'm going to be taken hostage again. But I don't want you worrying about me, or something that is going on with us and have that shift your focus in the split second that might be a matter of life and death." She tried a cocky smile, but her lips trembled and ruined it. "I might not always be there to save your ass like I was today."

He grinned, even as his eyes burned. "God, I love you."

She'd already opened her mouth to continue her terribly misguided defense of why they shouldn't be together. His sudden confession stopped her cold. "What did you just say?"

He closed the distance between them, unfolded her arms and put them around his waist. "I already think about you all the time. I worry about you—"

"Worry? Why? I can take care of—"

"I know. I meant in the general way a person does who loves another person. I wonder if the day is going well for you, how the meeting with the new client went. I find myself wanting to run this idea or that past you, get your take on things. I want to watch football with you, or even just watch you watch football. I want to stare into your eyes. For hours. Days." He lifted his hands to her face. "You've already moved into my head and into my heart. You're not a dangerous distraction to me as long as I can pick up the phone anytime I want and hear your voice, or know where you'll be come the end of the day." He kissed her slowly, fully, until they both ran short of breath. "The only way you'd be a danger to me is if you leave me. I don't think I could function with a broken heart."

A single tear slid down her cheek. "I can't believe Crybaby O'Keefe is making *me* cry. That was the most beautiful thing you just said."

He ran a finger across her lips, then dried the tear. "I love you, Terror Mahoney. I never had a clue what love was like until you barged back into my life."

She sniffled even as she lifted one eyebrow. "Barged?"

"Swaggered?"

"Why don't we say strolled and leave it at that?"

"I can live with strolled." He sobered and felt his heart climb into his throat. "Can you—" He had to stop and swallow it back down again. "Could you live with me, Erin? As my wife? Statistics be damned?"

Tears sprang to life in her eyes once again. "You're totally ruining my superwoman image here, Supercop."

He grinned, knowing his eyes were suspiciously damp, too. "Well, if you're really nice to me, I'll let you wear my red cape. Occasionally."

"I think I could be really nice to you."

"You think so?"

"It might take me a while to get really good at it though." That dry smile curved her lips. "Probably, oh, forty or fifty years. Maybe longer. I'm a perfectionist."

Brady's heart exploded inside his chest. Had she really just said yes? He swung her into his arms. "Would you like to get a head start right now?" She nodded and he was halfway to the bedroom when he stopped dead. "Wait a minute."

"What? What's wrong?"

He set her on her feet. "You haven't closed the deal."

"I haven't closed the— What?"

"Closed the deal. I believe in order to be binding, both parties have to sign on the dotted—"

She leaped at him, wrapping her legs around his waist. He caught her hard against his chest, barely keeping them both upright.

"I love you, Brady." She kissed him all over his face. "Is that what you needed to hear?"

It was better than anything he'd ever imagined. He'd absolutely found something worth bucking the statistics for. "Well, once is enough to close the deal, but—"

"I love you," she said softly, then kissed him long and slow, leaving no doubts about her feelings. "Now take me to bed so I can show you."

"Gladly."

She brushed his hair off his forehead. "And as foreplay, you can tell me what happened to Todd." At his shocked look, she merely smiled and said, "Hey, if I'm going to be a cop's wife, I'm going to have to learn to mix business with pleasure, right?''

"That's taking it a bit too far, but I do love you for trying. Have I told you how much I love you?''

"Why don't you show me?'' She kissed him again. "To hell with Todd, and business be damned. For a while anyway.''

"My thoughts exactly.''

_____Epilogue_____

ERIN LISTENED as the newscaster finished reporting on Todd's trial. Her phone rang a second later.

Brady's voice filled her ear. "Did you see?"

She instantly felt better. "Yeah," she said quietly. "I saw. I'm just glad it's over." It had been six months since Todd had held her and Gina at gunpoint. Everyone in the city knew the details by now. The Hans had been responsible for Sanderson's death. They'd tried to coerce him into allowing them to continue to run their black market porn business through the Laundromat. When he hadn't given in, they'd taken matters into their own hands.

Todd had tried to pump Bradford Pitts for information, hoping to conclusively tarnish Sanderson so they could condemn his underground actions while simultaneously expressing their shock and sorrow over his downfall. He'd planned to turn it around and actually use it as a campaign platform on organized crime. And if he'd cleared Sanderson, then that worked for the mayor, too, proving the police department was doing their job. Only the commissioner's job would have been at risk, which didn't bother Todd a bit. Todd, who had been promised a job as deputy mayor if the mayor won.

Even after Pitts's death he'd continued to have the Hans' activities surreptitiously monitored. What he hadn't counted on was the Hans discovering his nosing around. They'd told Todd he was next unless he pushed the mayor to favorably push some zoning changes in an area they were looking to build in. Todd had been more than willing to sell out the mayor to save his skin, but had panicked when he realized his power didn't extend to that level of political influence. He'd stalled. Then a zoning commissioner had turned up dead with all the evidence pointing to Todd. And he'd finally cracked.

He knew Brady would get the case, and because of Todd's past with Erin, he didn't think he'd get a fair shake. So, his logic dubious at best by then, he'd gone to Erin's office hoping to force Brady to listen to him. In the end he'd turned witness against the Hans and gotten immunity. Once a weasel, always a weasel.

"I actually got a call from Henley this morning," she told Brady, flicking the television off. "He offered me a job."

"You're kidding."

"Press secretary. Can you believe that?"

"Actually, I can. You can't help it if you're good at what you do, sweetheart. What did you say?"

"I gave Gina a shot at it since I'm not going near the world of politics for the foreseeable future. She turned him down cold."

"Smart girl. You two are going like gangbusters lately. Besides, you're a lot more fun to work with."

Erin curled up on in the corner of the couch. "You think so, do you? You being an authority on job fun."

"I know so. And my job is fun. For me anyway. Listen, speaking of my job, there's been a break in the Walters case that I need to follow up on."

"So you won't be here for dinner. No problem. 1 can still fix something and save it for you if you want." Only six months, but Erin was already well used to the routine.

"I was hoping I could persuade you to meet me at Jimmy's. I'll only have a few minutes, but we can grab a slice of pizza. Catch up."

She loved the routine. Because no matter how tied up the two of them were, and they both had their share of demands, they always made time for one another. It was like an addiction they were both more than willing to feed. For life. "I'll see if I can squeeze you in," she said. "But only because the Sixers are playing and the guys at Jimmy's need someone to remind them that we're heading for the championships this year no matter what the Bulls think."

"I'm sure they'll enjoy the lesson in humility."

"Besides," she added, "your mom called and she has more helpful ideas for the wedding."

Brady groaned. "No, please, not tonight."

"She has this cousin who knows this guy who is a friend of a guy who can do our silk flowers for wholesale. She has the whole color scheme all picked out. Again. She even found matching cummerbunds for the guys. My brothers will be so thrilled. Mauve being their color and all."

"Do they know this yet?"

"I am all that is standing between you and certain death. Strangulation by mauve cummerbund will probably be the M.O."

He sighed heavily and Erin tried hard not to be too amused at his expense. But he was pretty damn adorable when he tried not to let his mother wrap her big bad cop son around her little finger. Erin had already started taking notes.

"I'll do anything if you can get me out of that conversation and make this go away," he begged.

"Anything?"

"Yeah," he said, not sounding nearly so tortured all of a sudden. Perhaps he'd been taking a few notes of his own. "Anything."

"I think you might have a deal. Want to close it now or later?"

"Now. I love you, Erin."

"I love you, too, Supercop." She paused, then added, "But you'd better bring your red cape. You're going to need it."

COMING SOON...

AN EXCITING
OPPORTUNITY TO SAVE
ON THE PURCHASE OF
HARLEQUIN AND
SILHOUETTE BOOKS!

*DETAILS TO FOLLOW
IN OCTOBER 2001!*

YOU WON'T WANT TO MISS IT!

PHQ401

Harlequin truly does
make any time special....
This year we are celebrating
weddings in style!

A
Walk
Down
the Aisle
WEDDING CELEBRATION

To help us celebrate, we want you to tell us how wearing the Harlequin wedding gown will make your wedding day special. As the grand prize, Harlequin will offer one lucky bride the chance to **"Walk Down the Aisle"** in the Harlequin wedding gown!

There's more...

For her honeymoon, she and her groom will spend five nights at the **Hyatt Regency Maui.** As part of this five-night honeymoon at the hotel renowned for its romantic attractions, the couple will enjoy a candlelit dinner for two in Swan Court, a sunset sail on the hotel's catamaran, and duet spa treatments.

Maui • Molokai • Lanai

To enter, please write, in, 250 words or less, how wearing the Harlequin wedding gown will make your wedding day special. The entry will be judged based on its emotionally compelling nature, its originality and creativity, and its sincerity. This contest is open to Canadian and U.S. residents only and to those who are 18 years of age and older. There is no purchase necessary to enter. Void where prohibited. See further contest rules attached. Please send your entry to:

Walk Down the Aisle Contest

In Canada	In U.S.A.
P.O. Box 637	P.O. Box 9076
Fort Erie, Ontario	3010 Walden Ave.
L2A 5X3	Buffalo, NY 14269-9076

You can also enter by visiting www.eHarlequin.com
Win the Harlequin wedding gown and the vacation of a lifetime!
The deadline for entries is October 1, 2001.

HARLEQUIN®
Makes any time special ®

HARLEQUIN WALK DOWN THE AISLE TO MAUI CONTEST 1197
OFFICIAL RULES
NO PURCHASE NECESSARY TO ENTER

1. To enter, follow directions published in the offer to which you are responding. Contest begins April 2, 2001, and ends on October 1, 2001. Method of entry may vary. Mailed entries must be postmarked by October 1, 2001, and received by October 8, 2001.

2. Contest entry may be, at times, presented via the Internet, but will be restricted solely to residents of certain geographic areas that are disclosed on the Web site. To enter via the Internet, if permissible, access the Harlequin Web site (www.eHarlequin.com) and follow the directions displayed online. Online entries must be received by 11:59 p.m. E.S.T. on October 1, 2001.

    In lieu of submitting an entry online, enter by mail by hand-printing (or typing) on an 8½" x 11" plain piece of paper, your name, address (including zip code), Contest number/name and in 250 words or fewer, why winning a Harlequin wedding dress would make your wedding day special. Mail via first-class mail to: Harlequin Walk Down the Aisle Contest 1197, (in the U.S.) P.O. Box 9076, 3010 Walden Avenue, Buffalo, NY 14269-9076, (in Canada) P.O. Box 637, Fort Erie, Ontario L2A 5X3, Canada.

    Limit one entry per person, household address and e-mail address. Online and/or mailed entries received from persons residing in geographic areas in which Internet entry is not permissible will be disqualified.

3. Contests will be judged by a panel of members of the Harlequin editorial, marketing and public relations staff based on the following criteria:
    - Originality and Creativity—50%
    - Emotionally Compelling—25%
    - Sincerity—25%

    In the event of a tie, duplicate prizes will be awarded. Decisions of the judges are final.

4. All entries become the property of Torstar Corp. and will not be returned. No responsibility is assumed for lost, late, illegible, incomplete, inaccurate, nondelivered or misdirected mail or misdirected e-mail, for technical, hardware or software failures of any kind, lost or unavailable network connections, or failed, incomplete, garbled or delayed computer transmission or any human error which may occur in the receipt or processing of the entries in this Contest.

5. Contest open only to residents of the U.S. (except Puerto Rico) and Canada, who are 18 years of age or older, and is void wherever prohibited by law; all applicable laws and regulations apply. Any litigation within the Province of Quebec respecting the conduct or organization of a publicity contest may be submitted to the Régie des alcools, des courses et des jeux for a ruling. Any litigation respecting the awarding of a prize may be submitted to the Régie des alcools, des courses et des jeux only for the purpose of helping the parties reach a settlement. Employees and immediate family members of Torstar Corp. and D. L. Blair, Inc., their affiliates, subsidiaries and all other agencies, entities and persons connected with the use, marketing or conduct of this Contest are not eligible to enter. Taxes on prizes are the sole responsibility of winners. Acceptance of any prize offered constitutes permission to use winner's name, photograph or other likeness for the purposes of advertising, trade and promotion on behalf of Torstar Corp., its affiliates and subsidiaries without further compensation to the winner, unless prohibited by law.

6. Winners will be determined no later than November 15, 2001, and will be notified by mail. Winners will be required to sign and return an Affidavit of Eligibility form within 15 days after winner notification. Noncompliance within that time period may result in disqualification and an alternative winner may be selected. Winners of trip must execute a Release of Liability prior to ticketing and must possess required travel documents (e.g. passport, photo ID) where applicable. Trip must be completed by November 2002. No substitution of prize permitted by winner. Torstar Corp. and D. L. Blair, Inc., their parents, affiliates, and subsidiaries are not responsible for errors in printing or electronic presentation of Contest, entries and/or game pieces. In the event of printing or other errors which may result in unintended prize values or duplication of prizes, all affected game pieces or entries shall be null and void. If for any reason the Internet portion of the Contest is not capable of running as planned, including infection by computer virus, bugs, tampering, unauthorized intervention, fraud, technical failures, or any other causes beyond the control of Torstar Corp. which corrupt or affect the administration, secrecy, fairness, integrity or proper conduct of the Contest, Torstar Corp. reserves the right, at its sole discretion, to disqualify any individual who tampers with the entry process and to cancel, terminate, modify or suspend the Contest or the Internet portion thereof. In the event of a dispute regarding an online entry, the entry will be deemed submitted by the authorized holder of the e-mail account submitted at the time of entry. Authorized account holder is defined as the natural person who is assigned to an e-mail address by an Internet access provider, online service provider or other organization that is responsible for arranging e-mail address for the domain associated with the submitted e-mail address. **Purchase or acceptance of a product offer does not improve your chances of winning.**

7. Prizes: (1) Grand Prize—A Harlequin wedding dress (approximate retail value: $3,500) and a 5-night/6-day honeymoon trip to Maui, HI, including round-trip air transportation provided by Maui Visitors Bureau from Los Angeles International Airport (winner is responsible for transportation to and from Los Angeles International Airport) and a Harlequin Romance Package, including hotel accomodations (double occupancy) at the Hyatt Regency Maui Resort and Spa, dinner for (2) two at Swan Court, a sunset sail on Kiele V and a spa treatment for the winner (approximate retail value: $4,000); (5) Five runner-up prizes of a $1000 gift certificate to selected retail outlets to be determined by Sponsor (retail value $1000 ea.). Prizes consist of only those items listed as part of the prize. Limit one prize per person. All prizes are valued in U.S. currency.

8. For a list of winners (available after December 17, 2001) send a self-addressed, stamped envelope to: Harlequin Walk Down the Aisle Contest 1197 Winners, P.O. Box 4200 Blair, NE 68009-4200 or you may access the www.eHarlequin.com Web site through January 15, 2002.

Contest sponsored by Torstar Corp., P.O. Box 9042, Buffalo, NY 14269-9042, U.S.A.

PHWDACONT2

Brimming with passion and sensuality,
this collection offers two full-length
Harlequin Temptation novels.

Full Bloom

by *New York Times* bestselling author

JAYNE
—ANN—
KRENTZ

Emily Ravenscroft has had enough! It's time she took her life back,
out of the hands of her domineering family and Jacob Stone, the
troubleshooter they've always employed to get her out of hot water.
The new Emily—vibrant and willful—doesn't need Jacob to rescue
her. She needs him to love her, against all odds.

And

Compromising Positions

a brand-new story from bestselling author

VICKY LEWIS
THOMPSON

Look for it on sale September 2001.